HELLHOUND BOUND

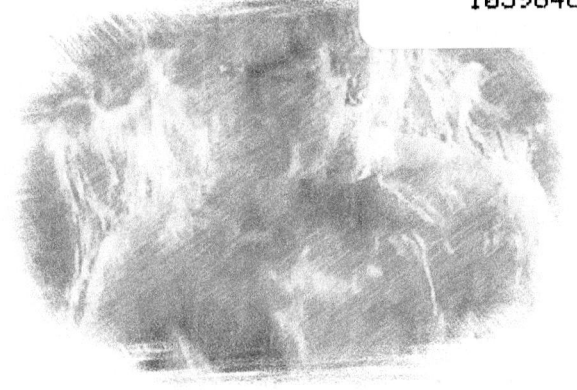

D. THOMAS JERLO

Foundations Publishing Company
Brandon, MS 39047
www.foundationsbooks.net

Hellbound Hound
By: D. Thomas Jerlo

Cover by: Dawné Dominique
Edited by: Steve Soderquist
Copyright 2018© D. Thomas Jerlo

Published in the United States of America
Worldwide Electronic & Digital Rights
Worldwide English Language Print Rights

ISBN: 978-1-64583-008-5

Acknowledgments:

*To Steve and Laura, whose hard work and dedication
to their authors knows no bounds.*

Chapter One

Sweet, pliable flesh squished between the recesses of his teeth followed by the usual ear-shattering shrieks.

They always screamed.

As the t'elan's blood splashed across his palate, the delectable taste of its cold terror at the realization of the inevitable settled into his consciousness. When the mortal took his last breath, he devoured every last piece of the human flesh.

What he liked best was when they fought back. Demented arousal, he called it. There was nothing better in this world—or the next.

It was a helluva job, but someone had to do it.

Rhune cracked open an eye. As usual, the memory of his nightly escapades faded into variegated scenes that never quite formed. The one constant: an intense sense of accomplishment. Not in fifteen hundred years had that changed. That, and the sins carried in the blood of his t'elans. That sour taste never went away.

The lifetimes ago when he'd lived in darkness and driven by blood he'd never truly known compassion, or love, for that matter. It took him two deaths and a sacred vow to keep his sorry ass out of Hell. Now his life—or rather his nights—consisted of hunting humans and delivering them to where they deserved to spend the rest of eternity.

The best thing about the job was the beginning of each day. He hadn't realized how much he'd missed sunrises, until that first morning when he saw the bright disk of light rise over the horizon, and he hadn't burst into flames. Since then, he rose with the sun, refusing to take such beauty for granted again.

Other than that, his life consisted of merely existing…and that was good enough for him.

The dead insect stain he stared at on the ceiling before his transformation never changed either.

Stupid wasp.

With the rising sun, One-Stop Joe's neon sign sparked bright for a second, then went out completely.

At least one thing still works around here.

And entirely his fault, too. The garage he'd built just south of I-18 and South Fork was over eighty years old, when cars were in the process of replacing horses. It was the only stop for thirty miles in any direction with picturesque prairie skies that chased fields of grasslands that changed color with every season.

When Rhune needed supplies, he trekked south to the small town of Rio Morden. In thirty-odd years or so, he'd start heading to North Bend, alternating between the two so that his agelessness wouldn't arouse suspicions. Folks had a tendency to wag tongues, no matter what era.

Part of his covenant was not to interact with the mortal race except for appearances' sake. The seven-odd centuries he'd been earthbound he'd never been lonely. The occasional supple bodies that would frequent his bed were always different women, and they'd be gone from his abode well before midnight.

There were no relationships. No ties. No love. Nothing that could emotionally bind him to this world.

He had a job to do. That was it. His heart was his own.

With the rustic gasoline pump, the garage's rundown appearance, and the four feet of grass he never cut, folks rarely stopped by. He'd made sure to build well off the beaten path. Few people saw his sign from I-18 and the poor souls that did stop were either lost, stupid, or both. He made sure to send them on their way well before dark. After these many centuries, his existence was what he made it.

Quiet.

Isolated.

Home.

He rose from the bed and stretched, flexing muscles he never had to work to maintain. The pile of clothes hidden beneath yet another pile of dirty clothes caught his eye.

"Time to order more, I suppose," he mumbled.

After a quick shower and a bowl of cornflakes with milk on the cusp of curdling, he changed into a pair of somewhat clean jeans and a t-shirt before heading out the screen door. The sound that followed was that of a tortured banshee.

I should oil that, he thought for the hundredth time. *Yeah, and maybe today the damn pump will work.*

The moment he stepped outside, something stopped him in his tracks. He shifted right. Then left. The world smelled...wrong. Almost corrupted—and he knew a lot about corruption.

A glint of metal caught the morning sunlight as a car drove by in the distance on I-18. His line of vision followed the vehicle even though he couldn't see it through the grass that grew in wild abandon on his property. Whispers of danger slipped through the air and wound around him. He sensed a change about to happen.

Rhune didn't like change. So many years of staunch habits were difficult to break. So why was intuition coaxing him toward the town of Rio Morden?

He pushed the notion from his mind and went in search of a hose that hopefully wouldn't leak.

Chapter Two

Hanna could have sworn she looked both ways before braving the busy intersection, but when the sudden blast of a car horn sounded, she panicked. The heel of her shoe snagged in the asphalt and down she went. Hard. With no time to stop and take injury inventory she bound to her feet, her lungs aching for air, and continued running. Only then did she brave a look at the palms of her hands. Apparently, running and picking pebbles from out of her flesh was likened to walking and chewing gum; it wasn't just a cliché with her. She tripped and almost went down again. Fire swept through her palms as she steadied herself against a concrete wall.

I'm going to be late. Again. Thank God it's Friday.

She pushed her way through the glass doors of Cordelle's District Attorney's Office and stopped at the corner of the corridor. Seeing Tiffany wasn't at the reception desk, Hanna heaved a sigh of relief and hurried to her desk at the back of the building's first-floor cubicles. Nice and secluded. In seconds she was booting up her computer.

"Late again are we, Ms. Carmichael?"

The forced saccharine tone made her stiffen. Even the woman's name was sickeningly sweet. Tiffany Hyatt. The beautiful Mulatto bitch with ice-blue eyes and a disposition uglier than sin. Wearing her usual skin-tight skirt and top, Tiffany looked to be auditioning for an X-rated movie rather than being the receptionist of a law office, and because the skirt was below her knees and the blouse expensive silk, she got away with wearing such ridiculous outfits. There was never too much revealed, but enough to make imaginations run wild.

Hanna glared at the receptionist, hoping it conveyed the 'you're not the boss of me' look it had meant to inspire. "It wasn't my fault. The bus driver blew by my stop. I had to run eight blocks back."

Unfortunately, Tiffany's condescending scowl won the fuck-off prize. "Let's hope no one else noticed," she murmured before sashaying away from Hanna's desk.

Sure, you witch. You're running to tell someone right now.

A receptionist with an attitude. Go figure. Also, one who happened to be fucking one of the attorneys. *Which* attorney was the million dollar question.

Darla's chubby face popped over the top of her cubicle. "You should follow her. Then we'll know who she's shagging."

Hanna shook her head with a pout. "She hates me. It's as simple as that. Maybe I ran over her dog in a past life or something."

"Well, do it right next time. Run *her* over!" They shared a fit of uncontrollable giggles.

"She's just jealous. She wants your eyes, so beware. If she's anywhere near you when you're sleeping, make sure you leave one of them open. I don't trust that bitch."

Hanna immediately looked to the floor whenever someone mentioned her eyes, but not before she saw Darla stick her tongue in her cheek and pump her hand beside it.

Darla was her one and only friend in the world, but she didn't have time for this. Four accordion file folders bursting with documents leaned against the side of her computer screen; folders she had to go through page by page, word for word for a trial scheduled next Tuesday. Not to mention the two storage boxes of exhibits that needed stamping.

Before she got caught fornicating the dog by 'I'm You're Boss, Tiffany the Porn Star,' she shooed Darla away. "I gotta work if I'm going to get this done and filed in court by Monday morning."

Without any regard for her personal space, Darla skittered around the cubicle wall and parked herself on the corner of Hanna's desk. She leaned close and whispered, "Why are you busting your ass for this company? You're going to be working all weekend again, and for what? Four weeks' holiday? Big fucking deal. You've earned it. For all the overtime you put in here, you should be getting a week in Jamaica paid for by them. Why do you it? Thirty-five grand a year? They walk all over you like you're a rug and you continue busting your ass for them. Hell, the fucking receptionist thinks she's your boss, for Christ's sake. You deserve better."

"Um, you work here too, Darla, and with my Christmas bonuses from the two other lawyers I work for it's almost forty, thank you very much."

"You're too smart. You should be working for the big boys, like Dellon, Smith & West. Just saying."

Darla's round bottom promptly disappeared around the corner as she headed to her own cubicle.

The truth stung. So what if she was content here? Hanna did her job from eight to four, then went home, ate, and slept...kind of. She was an introvert and for her, sleep was a commodity. Especially for an insomniac.

With a sigh, Hanna pulled out a stack of witness statements. She began sorting through them alphabetically and then dividing them into the dates they'd be called to give their evidence. The defendant's brother, Rick Andrews, was first.

She settled into the tedious job of reading and note-taking. Three transcripts and five witness folders later, the blinking message light on her phone caught her eye.

He always called directly to voicemail.

She keyed in her security code and listened to the emotionless voice.

"Hanna, come and see me."

She hung up the receiver and wondered for the umpteenth time whether Stan Winford, lawyer extraordinaire, was half-robot. All he did was work, and he didn't like to be kept waiting.

With pad of paper and pen in hand, she headed to the elevators.

Surely she hadn't heard him right. "You want me to go where?"

"Rio Morden. A new witness has come forward. His name's Roger Simmons. He claims to have seen the defendant walking along the fringe of the resort's golf course about a half hour after the fire had been set. If that's the case, then Frank wasn't where he said he was. It destroys his alibi."

Their trial was a tricky one. Adam Drysdale, a respected lawyer in the legal community, had been found shot in his burnt lakeside cottage almost two years before. Frank Andrews had been arrested shortly after that. He'd been a former client of Drysdale's, who apparently hadn't liked the verdict Drysdale got for him. Mr. Winford had taken the case on with a vengeance and was determined to put the guy responsible for his best friend's murder behind bars.

"But that's over three hundred miles away!" Hanna knew how lame she sounded even before the whine left her lips, but what Mr. Winford was asking went over and above the call of paralegal duty, even for her. Every witness in this case had been personally interviewed by him. Why her? And why now? And days before the start of the trial?

The out-of-date family photograph on his desk caught her eye. His wife and ten-year-old daughter looked as starched as he did. *No wonder he works all the time,* she thought.

Hanna had learned that Mrs. Winford had suffered a grave accident some time ago and was now confined to a wheelchair, unable to walk or talk. *Maybe working is his way of dealing with the tragedy,* she mused.

Winford's next words cut through her thoughts. "I've rented a car for you. There's one motel in town. The Mercury Inn, I think it's called. Tiffany's booked you a room there."

Obviously, he hadn't heard any of her protests, but maybe this wasn't such a bad idea. At least she'd have wheels for the weekend. "Who's going to prepare the depositions?"

"Sondra."

Her mouth dropped. "She's been articling for what, a month? Has she done any litigation?"

"She has to learn somehow," he clipped, cutting off any further protest. "Look, I chose you because you're patient, soft-spoken, and however strange they are, your eyes have a calming effect."

She focused on the carpet.

"I've talked with this guy a couple of times. He's skittish. I want him comfortable. I want him to be forthcoming in his evidence. I want him to feel safe. I want every detail, including what he saw the defendant wearing that night. Did he hear him fart? Everything. We'll call him last, so don't add him to the witness list just yet. I have another engagement this weekend or I'd go myself. And one very important thing. Tell no one about where you're going and who you're going to see."

"Why?"

"He's our cincher in the case. We're going to get a conviction because of Simmons' testimony. I want no one knowing about him until we have his statement in hand. Understand?"

She nodded. What did she have planned anyway? Diddly-squat, that's what. Who knows? This trip could turn out to be an adventure. A mini-vacation, even. Hell, she might find Prince Charming along the side of the road. But who was she kidding. She'd have better luck winning the lottery. With her weeks filled with her day job and the weekends spent *trying* to sleep, having a love life wasn't an option. And the few one-night stands Hanna experienced were nothing more than not wanting to die a virgin. In her view, relationships were way too much work for too little gain.

At least she didn't have trial work to contend with.

"When do I leave?" she mumbled.

"Tomorrow morning. Make sure you get those files to Sondra."

"Can I go home early to get ready?"

One of Winford's eyebrows rose a smidgen higher than the other.

Hanna's cheeks instantly blistered with heat. "I take it that's a no." She rose from the chair and almost ran from his office.

It took more than an hour to put the files back into some sort of coherent order, and the two trips it took for her to drop off the boxes elicited nothing more than a distracted bob of Sondra's head. Not even a thank you.

Everyone ignored her. Except Tiffany, of course.

"Take this. Here's some water, dear. It'll make you feel better."

Her mother's face suddenly loomed inches away. Hanna had almost forgotten what she'd looked like.

Almost.

Wake up!

She tried to refuse the medication, but without a will of her own, she saw her hand reach out and take the pink spotted pills, just like the good girl she always is.

"Now you get some sleep. No more of this nonsense."

"Yes, mama," she heard herself say.

That had been their routine. Bath time. Brush teeth. Take pills. Sleep.

Blackness. No dreams.

Wake up!

Her dreamworld shifted. Hanna now strolled through a beautiful summer field. The world felt surreal; so bright and free, unlike the chemically induced fog of her childhood. If the authorities had known her mother had kept her pacified with drugs, Hanna knew she'd have grown up differently. Maybe she'd be a lawyer instead of a paralegal. Too consumed with her job and getting her own beauty sleep, her mother had literally stolen her childhood. Hanna's insomnia had become a dirty little secret she talked about only with shrinks.

But not the drugs. She never discussed the pills her mother gave her.

"If you tell anyone," her mother used to warn, *"they'll take you away from me. You'll live in an orphanage, or with a bunch of strange foster families."*

Those words lingered in her ears as the beautiful dream she was in darkened. Storm clouds rolled in. Thunder rumbled ominously in the distance.

Wake up!

Hanna woke and untangled herself from the sheets for the fourth time that night. The takeout burger she'd wolfed down for dinner wasn't sitting right. Whether it was excitement or anticipation of the trip, sleep was playing tag with her. She prayed this wasn't the beginning of another session of sleep deprivation. Why couldn't she catch a few winks like a normal person?

The years her mother would put her down to nap, only to wake up screaming, would have sent anyone over the edge. But her mother was of a different ilk, as she was fond of saying. She fought Hanna's illness with illicit drugs as steadfastly as Hanna battled with going to sleep. When total exhaustion or those horrid pink, spotted pills sent her into a deep unconsciousness, she was safe. Nothing could touch her.

It wasn't until her mother's death that she'd finally kicked the drug habit. Thank goodness for school. Long nights of studying proved conducive to her insomnia. Her studies had kept her sane, and those endless hours of pouring through those books had her at the head of her class.

At eighteen, she landed the paralegal job in the district attorney's office. During the exhaustive days and evenings of working on litigious lawsuits, she managed to catch at least four to five hours of sleep a night. Those were the good nights.

When she closed her eyes for the fifth time, something chased her through the darkness.

Something massive.

Something with fiery, glowing eyes that both fascinated and scared the shit out of her. Something she hadn't dreamed about since she was a child.

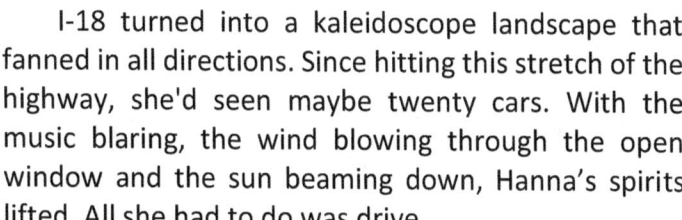

I-18 turned into a kaleidoscope landscape that fanned in all directions. Since hitting this stretch of the highway, she'd seen maybe twenty cars. With the music blaring, the wind blowing through the open window and the sun beaming down, Hanna's spirits lifted. All she had to do was drive.

No turn offs.

No streetlights.

No people.

Some ten miles later the car suddenly jerked and almost stalled. She'd topped up the gas tank when stopping for that one washroom break, so it couldn't be that. She slowed down and listened. When it didn't happen again, she turned the radio back up and carried on.

Chapter Three

Rhune twisted the wrench to tighten the bolt, but it was at such an awkward angle the tool slipped in his sweat-soaked hand which caused his knuckles to scrape along the rusty metal edge he hadn't bothered to hammer down.

"Curva!"

Blood spurted. The cut was deep. He shrugged and continued working. Seconds later, the wound healed. He wiped the residual blood from his hand down the side of his jeans to add to the stains already there.

He'd replaced the main hose a few years back, yet this was inevitable. It was time for a new one, which meant he'd have to head into town, his least favorite thing to do. If not for him needing to pump gas for his bike and truck, he'd have thrown the part away and not thought twice about it.

Rio Morden consisted of one main road, two restaurants, one of which was also a gas station, and a motel. Quaint, with a small population like North Bend.

He made a stop at the one and only hardware store. Luckily, Ben Hardy, the second grandson owner of Hardy's Hardware, found a five-foot hose buried deep in the back of the storeroom. Rhune thanked him, tossed a twenty at the cash register, and left without waiting for his change. He wasn't one to jaw with townsfolk, however, they knew him by his jalopy and usually waved or nodded hello when they saw him.

He opened the door of his truck, the old hinges screeching across the parking lot. *I should oil that,* he thought for the second time that week, then promptly forgot.

He put the engine into gear, checked his mirrors and backed out. The jolt forward wasn't noticeable but the clunk that followed was. He slammed the truck into park and got out.

Behind him was a dark blue Volvo. Where it'd been a second ago was beyond him. He'd checked all three mirrors.

A young woman's stunned, pale face stared back through the windshield. She fumbled with the door and exited. Bright spots of color peppered her otherwise flawless cheeks. "D-Didn't you see me?"

He sensed her trying not to scream. Then an odd turbulence rolled through his system, similar to earlier that morning. He took a deep breath and blew it out slowly.

What was that? he wondered, and pushed the thought away when he realized she still waited for an answer. "I looked before I backed out. You weren't there unless you were directly behind me, in which case you should have seen my reverse lights, not to mention the warning beeps my truck makes. That sound, by the way, means someone is backing up."

Subtle curls the color of molasses that reached to her shoulders caught the sunlight. Her face, though at the moment the pallor of chalk, was unpretentiously pretty with full, pink lips. She looked everywhere but at him.

He headed to the back of his truck and discovered the Volvo's fender on the asphalt.

Her voice came out one octave away from being a shriek. "How do I explain this to the rental place? Or my boss?"

There was an innocence about her that he didn't see too often in people these days. Life was quick to harden most, but it seemed not her. Of medium height and weight, she could have turned more heads if she didn't dress like some uptight secretary. His gaze traveled down the length of her modest skirt to her beautifully defined bare legs and sensible heels.

"I knew this day was too good to be true." He heard panic in her voice.

As he focused on her face, he couldn't understand why she wouldn't look at him. "Hey, I'm sorry. I swear I didn't see you. I own a garage down I-18. I'll tow your car there and fix it. Free of charge." Stunned by what he just said, he snapped his mouth shut.

She looked at least in his direction, but not at his face. "Excuse me?"

There was a garage in town, so why'd he open his trap and make such an offer? If he couldn't get it fixed by nightfall, he risked her being stuck out there.

With him.

Alone.

"Turn over the engine," he muttered.

She scrambled back into the car and turned the ignition. The car choked, coughed for a second, and then died. Absolute fear blazed across her face.

Who the hell's her boss? Satan? He refrained from smirking.

She leaned out the window, staring at the ground. "I have to be back in the city by Monday morning. There's a trial starting on Tuesday. I have to be there."

Fabulous! A lawyer. Couldn't I have fender-bendered a member of the Russian Mafia instead? Well, he got her into this mess, it was only right he help her out of it. "Let me take you and your car back to my garage where I can—"

"Are you nuts?"

"Apparently so," Rhune replied.

"I'm not going anywhere with you."

"Then stay here at the motel tonight. My treat. I'll bring the car back to you tomorrow good as new. The rental place won't even know there was an accident."

She exited the car slowly. "I'm supposed to trust you? Someone I've just met two minutes ago?"

"I swear I'm not some serial killer or rapist. Ben knows me," he added reluctantly.

"Oh, that makes me feel so much better. Who's Ben?" She zeroed in on the old-fashioned writing emblazoned on the side of his truck that was barely visible through the rust.

He tilted his head to the storefront behind him. "Ben Hardy."

A bit of skepticism melted from her face. "Hardy's Hardware?"

"Yeah. For the record, are *you* nuts?"

"No," she snipped.

She was like a Christmas tree. Every few seconds she changed colors.

He pursed his lips and headed inside, the clicking of her heels following not far behind. He resisted taking a second look. He had to admit those were the prettiest set of legs he'd seen in a long time.

The scenario inside the store turned into 'how to confuse someone in less than five seconds.' Ben Hardy barely knew him, except as some random customer who came in every couple of months for supplies. It took only a few minutes before they left the poor man scratching his head behind the counter. At least Ben had vouched for him.

Why did Rhune feel sorry for this woman? And why did she seem familiar? Sure, the rental car needed work, but for some reason every time he looked in her direction, she trembled. And not in the way most women normally did. Fear was something he knew a lot about, and she possessed buckets of it.

Obviously, a part had jarred loose in the engine when they hit. No biggie. He'd fix it, then the bumper, followed by sending her on her way. No one would be the wiser.

He reached his truck and opened the passenger door for her.

She stopped dead. "Um, no. That's not going to happen." She crossed her arms and stared at her shoes.

"What's your problem now?" His gaze lingered on her breasts far longer than it should have. Yep. Those were another two fine qualities she possessed.

"You expect me to get in your truck and drive to who knows where with you?"

Grinding his teeth, he jutted his chin toward the store. "What was all that about in there then?"

"Reassurance. You take my car and bring it back to me tomorrow. If you don't, I'll have the police at your door so fast with a list of charges you won't see daylight for a very long time. A business card, please."

She held out her hand and glared at his worn steel-toed boots.

"Fine," he forced out from between clenched teeth. He pulled out his wallet and fished through it until he found a tattered business card he'd had since the early eighties and handed it to her.

She snatched for the card. "I won't go to the authorities to make an accident report until after you deliver the car back. If I'm satisfied that no one can tell there's damage, then I might forego making a formal police statement. I'd rather not have to explain this to my boss, or the rental place. Got it?"

Without a backward glance, she turned and started down Main Street toward The Mercury Inn.

He watched as she walked away before lowering the yoke on the back of his truck, securing the chains and hoisted the car up. Rhune was almost home before he realized he hadn't even asked her her name. Well, there was only one motel in town. He'd be able to find her.

Definitely an emotional woman, he mused. Still, it was more than that. Every time he thought about her a chill chased down his spine—and not in a good way.

He managed to fix the fender in under an hour. After he lifted the hood and began checking the engine he discovered worn grooves on the head of the ignition fuse. It was a small wonder the vehicle hadn't broken down on the side of the road in the middle of nowhere. He replaced it and inspected every part to ensure the car would be safe to drive. By the time he finished, it was nearing midnight.

With grease still on his hands, Rhune chowed down on a crusty tuna casserole he'd made the night before. He left the dishes in the sink, brushed his teeth, and trudged to bed to stare at the insect stain on the ceiling, waiting for the inevitable to happen.

Chapter Four

Hanna's nerves were stretched to their limits and playing interference with the infuriating woman behind the hotel desk was beginning to push her over the edge. The Gladys Kraveth look-a-like asked a lot of questions, most of which she wasn't in the mood to answer. Her neck was sore, she was covered in road dust, and her mouth tasted like someone had crapped in it. Hanna wanted a bath and a bed, and not particularly in that order.

"Do you have a habit of entertaining men at late hours?"

Her mouth dropped. "I do not! And it's none of your damn business if I do. Just give me the registrar to sign, for goodness sake."

Finally, with her overnight bag in hand Hanna stopped in front of room 30, the last door down the hall by the fire exit. After three attempts, the key finally worked.

"By the way, my name's Mrs. Grady," the woman at the front desk called out. "If you need anything, let me know."

"Like hell I will, you nosey bitch," she grumbled under her breath.

Once inside, Hanna kicked off her heels, hung up her suit, and jumped into the shower. Minutes later, she was in her pajamas and lying on the bed, staring at the ceiling fan. Her head pounded in perfect succession with the rotation of the blades. If she didn't know better, she'd swear she had a touch of sunstroke.

Probably caused by tow-truck guy. Damn, he was hot. In both ways.

Everything had gone well taking Roger's statement, although he seemed more engrossed in gawking at her boobs than giving his evidence.

Mr. Winford had been right. Roger swore he'd seen Frank walking south along the golf course at about four in the morning. When she'd asked him what he was doing out there at that time of night, Roger said he'd gone to the lake for a late-night swim to straighten out. He'd been out partying by himself, but the way he'd said it gave her the creeps. However, he had described what Frank had been wearing, which was exactly what he was wearing when he'd been brought in for questioning. Roger couldn't have known that without being there; those details had never been released to the public. Forensics did find a chemical on Frank's t-shirt that could have been used as an accelerant, but nothing concrete. Also, there was no blood or gun residue on his clothes. Those facts made their case weak. With Roger as their star witness, they now had an excellent chance at a conviction.

Frank could have made it to Sage Creek, where the filthy rich and famous vacationed the summer months away in mansion-sized cottages, shot Drysdale, set the fire, and Roger spotted him walking back at four in the morning.

Forensics couldn't say for certain when Drysdale had died, as his body had been so severely burned, but they knew without a doubt that the fire that had engulfed his lakeside cottage had been set at approximately three-thirty in the morning. It fit the timeframe perfectly. They now had a witness that placed Frank in the vicinity of the crime scene.

But something about Roger felt off to her...way off. When she'd asked why he hadn't come forward sooner he just sneered with a shrug. That twist of his lips had made her skin crawl. He had told her that he'd read about the upcoming trial in the newspaper and called Mr. Winford directly.

The more Hanna thought about Roger the sicker she felt. She shivered and pulled up a blanket from the end of the bed, then reached for her cell and left a message for Mr. Winford, telling him the interview was done and she'd be back Sunday night. Being stuck in Rio Morden without a car certainly didn't turn into the mini-vacation she'd hoped for. Then again, nothing in her life went as planned. Tow-truck guy had better keep his promise about fixing the rental without anyone being able to detect the damage.

And talk about a Prince Charming in rags. The guy was so damn gorgeous she couldn't look at him without blushing. He dressed like a hobo, but oh boy, he filled out those rags beautifully. And why did he emanate heat like a furnace whenever she stood near him?

Because you can't stop internally combusting when you're around good-looking men, that's why, you idiot, she thought, blushing again despite her being alone.

Sudden realization kicked in.

I didn't even ask his name, for crying out loud!

All the business card said was *One-Stop Joe's* and a telephone number she couldn't make out because the printing had worn away. She should have looked at it before leaving in such a hissy-fit.

After she finished berating herself for her stupidity, she closed her eyes and dozed. When the sudden peal of the motel's phone jumped-started her awake, she reached for the receiver and rubbed the sleep from her eyes.

"Hello?"

"Ms. Carmichael?"

Half-expecting the nasal drawl of Mr. Winford, she cringed when she recognized the voice. "Yes?"

"It's Roger. Roger Simmons."

"Yes, I know. How did you know where I'd be?"

"There's only one hotel in town."

"Right. What can I do for you?"

"I know it's late and all, but..." A long pause followed.

"Yes?"

"Can you meet me?"

She glanced at the clock on the desk across from the bed.

It's almost twelve-thirty. What the hell?

"It's a bit late for a meeting. Can it wait 'til morning?"

"I know, I know, and I'm sorry, but there's something I forgot to tell you. Something important."

Hanna slid to the side of the bed and grabbed a pad of paper and a pen from her open briefcase. "Tell me now. I'll come by tomorrow morning and have you sign it."

"No. That old coot who owns the place is a nosy bitch."

Well, she couldn't argue with that. That woman's keenness to know just about everything was a little unnerving. Was it possible for Mrs. Grady to eavesdrop on their conversation?

Hanna refused to have this deposition screwed up. Mr. Winford wanted no one to know. Plus, Roger sounded scared. It was a small town. Everyone knew everyone, right? What harm could come from meeting with him?

As if reading her thoughts, Roger gave her directions. "Daly's Diner is open all night. When you leave the hotel, turn left and cut down the back lane. Hang another left at the end of it. You can't miss it. It's right on the corner. I'll be there in fifteen minutes." The line went dead.

"I'm billing Stan the Man extra for this," she grumbled and got up and dressed.

Thankfully, Mrs. Grady was nowhere in sight when she left. In fact, the front desk looked closed.

She gripped her briefcase tight and went out, looking both ways. Main Street was as deserted as the motel. The streetlights were on, but they weren't very bright. *Weird,* she thought. *Small town mentality to conserve energy, I suppose.*

Hanna followed the sidewalk to the back lane and peered down the shadowed alleyway. *What can happen?* The moment the thought entered her head it was as if the night grew darker, heavier; like in her nightmares. Her heartbeat quickened.

She swallowed hard and stepped into the alley. She had only made it halfway through when a calloused hand slapped over her mouth. In her sudden shock her briefcase slipped from her grasp. Strong arms dragged her deeper into the shadows. There, cold fingers snaked around her throat and promptly cut off her oxygen. The hand squeezed—then squeezed harder. Darkness began curtailing her sight. The stench of *something* filled the air. It was so caustic and strong it singed her nose hairs.

She tried to scream but couldn't.

Her nose burned.

The wild beating of her heart pulsated in her ears.

Her lungs screamed for air.

Darkness closed in as the fingers tightened even more around her larynx. A flash of red suddenly cut through her fading eyesight. Vaguely aware of an unearthly growl quaking in the concrete beneath her feet, she felt the grip around her throat loosen before falling away completely.

Something shoved her hard into the wall. The back of her head smacked into the bricks.

Half-turning, half-stumbling, Hanna tried to focus and breathe. She wiped at the tears in her eyes while the skin around her neck stung and crawled at the same time. Dazed and confused, she heard a strangled scream. One thing was for certain, it hadn't come from her. She squinted through the gloom—then wished she'd been knocked out cold.

What she saw couldn't be real. She was having one of her nightmares. But in those dreams her nose never felt like it was bleeding or her throat so raw that it felt like it had been scrubbed with steel wool. She tried to fight the panic eroding her world of reality, or what was left of it.

It wasn't a wolf or a dog, but it was part of that animal kingdom...sort of. Furry scales covered every inch of its massive body but they looked more like pliable, flaming metal that danced in slow motion, just like how fire moved. Its paws somewhat resembled those of a dog, but the back carpal pads were talons about five inches long and three inches thick. Its head was huge, its snout elongated, rather than wide. It stood about seven and a half feet tall and had a reddish glow emanating around its rigid, muscular frame. Heat radiated off it like a massive bonfire.

She inched her way slowly along the wall toward the street. If she'd had the power to be invisible, now would have been a good time to use it. The illumination of teeth larger than any Jaws poster gorged into the man who'd attacked her, who she happened to glimpse was Roger, or rather, what was left of him. His gurgling screams tapered into silence as his head detached from his body and fell with a resounding *plop* to the cement.

Blood had gushed in every direction. The flesh became mangled mush. Transfixed, she watched as this...*thing*...ate him. Head and all.

Collapsing to her knees, she tried to breathe. Instead, she gagged and dry-heaved with an ugly retching sound.

The monster paused, lifting its nose and sniffed at the air. It turned toward her, its fiery-filled eye sockets drilling straight into her.

She couldn't move; she couldn't think.

The beast took a step closer, still sniffing at the air. *It doesn't see me?*

The creature lowered its head and raised its haunches. With a snarl that rumbled down the entire alleyway, it advanced.

Before she passed out and died, which she was pretty sure was about to happen, tow-truck guy suddenly stood in front of her. She managed one last coherent thought before fainting away.

Why does he look like Casper the Ghost?

Chapter Five

Rhune's transformation had occurred like on any other ordinary night, but this out-of-body experience was something completely new. Never had this happened in all his centuries.

There was no delirious intervention; no x-ray like glimpses; no thick, coppery mist. He had simply stood there in the alley tearing apart his t'elan in order to devour the soul for delivery to Hell.

And *she* stood there watching it all. He remembered her now. Damn straight, he did.

When she collapsed to the street, he barely reached her in time.

In this hellish realm, he'd never *felt*. Then again, he'd never been both himself and the hellhound, either. As he held her in his arms, her essence soaked into him like rain.

Rationalizing this would take too long. He had to get her out of here and ponder the how and why later. When he lifted her off the ground, the beast's blazing gaze leveled on him.

Those are my eyes! But it wasn't him looking out through them.

He laid the woman gently on the ground and straightened. Somehow, he had to reintegrate with the hound. This certainly gave a whole new meaning to 'taking a good look at oneself.'

They circled. They sniffed the air at the same time. They narrowed their eyes exactly the same way – mirror images – but not.

"You will not harm her," he warned the hellhound.

The beast stopped and tilted his head, hearing something Rhune didn't.

Rhune bent and gathered the woman into his arms again. He took a couple of steps down the alley, then bolted for the street. When he rounded the corner, he stumbled to a stop. Every streetlight was out.

"What the...?"

There was no time to think about it. He made for the motel, past the vacant front desk and down the hall. He didn't have to look far to find her room. The last door by the fire escape had been kicked in. Peering down at her innocent face, he wondered what she'd done to deserve this.

He had no idea how they'd arrived at his gas station. One minute he was standing at the entrance of her motel room door, the next, he was in his living room. Every inch of his flesh tingled and burned. In his need to get her to safety, he must have intinctively invoked some kind of spell to get them out of there. Obviously, he still possessed his magic in this altered state.

After he placed her on his ratty couch, he resisted an inexplicable urge to drop to his knees and hold her tight.

The human who'd attacked her in the alley had wanted her dead. That much he'd gleaned in the first few seconds after he'd arrived and before the shock set in. His t'elan that night had been her attacker. Coincidence? Gambling had never been his *forte*, but he'd have bet his gas station that it wasn't happenstance.

She stirred, then her eyes fluttered and somewhat opened.

He stumbled back, stunned. When they had first met, he'd never noticed them. Then again, she'd looked everywhere but at him. Their intensity left him speechless, just as they always had before. They sparkled like gems. Multifaceted hues of indigo, green, yellow, and hazel seared into his soul. He'd never seen a human with such eyes before, at least not on this plane of existence. Then her lids slid closed.

It'd been a long time since he'd last seen them.

Running a hand over his shorn hair he glanced at the clock on the kitchen wall, which showed three thirty-five. Maybe later he'd be better able to understand it all. Right now, he was totally befuddled. Where had the hellhound gone? They didn't have friends. It was the nature of the beast. But the one in the alley? It had been distorted, changed somehow. It had been him, but it wasn't.

Knowing the danger she was in, could he let her go? And what if that biggest threat was him?

He was careful not to rouse her as he covered her with his favorite flannel blanket. Confounded to the core, he watched her sleep for a few minutes more.

A mere mortal. So pale and fragile. Does she know she's a Dreamwalker?

And is that all she is?

He trudged to bed, his head pounding with questions he had no answers to. After he settled into his blankets, Rhune stared at that dead insect stain on the ceiling until One-Stop Joe's neon sign blinked once and went out completely.

Chapter Six

Blood-curdling screams forced her to wake.

Shivering and bathed in sweat, her heart racing a hundred miles a second, Hanna leaped off the couch. With no idea if those screams had been hers or not, she stared frantically about the unfamiliar living room, decorated circa 1970 Kmart except for the big-ass, fifty-seven-inch flat screen TV. Wherever she was, this was definitely a guy's place.

The previous night slipped through her thoughts in foggy bits and pieces. She tried focusing past the pounding in her head, still everything remained incoherent fragments.

She gripped the blanket tight around her shoulders and did a desperate three-sixty. A pile of dirty dishes stacked haphazardly in a sink with several flies nose-diving into the filth caught her attention.

Through the dingy kitchen window above it dawn had crested with the most stunning mosaic streaks of bright oranges, reds and blues she'd ever seen. The vividness of colors against the towering stalks of uncut grass struck her dumb. She pinched herself to make sure it was real. Beyond the sunrise, prairie farmland stretched out as far as the eye could see.

Had she been kidnapped? The last thing she remembered was watching TV in the motel, and then, yes, the phone call. Who'd contacted her?

She decided it didn't matter where she was, it was time to leave. She dropped the blanket and tiptoed to the front door. Once she gripped the door handle, she pushed slowly. The hinges shrieked like a cat being tortured. Hannah stopped, listened, and studied the tattered screen that looked like a Pollock abstract but instead of paint, it was an artistic arrangement of a variety of squished bugs. Early morning light glinted off an old-fashioned gas pump about a hundred yards away. Above the station's canopy, a faded neon sign read *One-Stop Joe's*.

Tow-truck guy?

He lied! He was indeed a serial rapist-killer, drug-maniac, or at the very least, a kidnapper.

He drugged me and brought me here. Oh my GOD.

She held her breath as she painstakingly inched the screen door open. What felt like an hour later, she finally stepped outside. Peeled paint chips from the exterior porch crunched underfoot. Without thinking, she let go of the door which promptly slammed behind her. She jumped and choked down a scream.

The flash of chrome from a passing car glinted in the corner of her eye. She recognized I-18 in the distance. Hell, she'd driven past here yesterday on her way to Rio Morden and never even noticed this place. It'd been only yesterday, right? When would people stop drugging her?

She waited on the front step, counting the seconds. When no other cars passed, she made her way toward the highway.

"Good morning."

She screamed and lurched around. Tow-truck guy stood framed beneath the decrepit doorway, his feet bare and wearing nothing but a pair of gray sweatpants. Her jaw dropped while the rest of her scream lodged firmly in her throat. His tousled hair and pronounced six-pack completed the package way too perfectly.

How can he look better than yesterday? The large tattoo that covered most of his chiseled chest and stomach fascinated her. It depicted a screaming skull amidst scrolling designs and at the bottom on both sides were old-fashioned keys.

When she realized she stood there like a dolt with her mouth hanging open, she promptly dropped her gaze. "Where am I? Why did you bring me here? Why did you drug and kidnap me? I'm going to have your ass arrested and hauled into prison for a very long time."

He *hmphed* something that sounded a lot like *bullshit*. "You don't remember?"

She peered at him through slips of her hair. For a second, he looked relieved—almost.

"I don't remember..." Intense pain suddenly exploded inside her skull. She fell to her knees, gasping. Visions of red splashes like paint strewn across a canvas filled her mind's eye. The events of the previous night crashed home.

She couldn't breathe.

She couldn't move.

She couldn't stop the horror repeatedly playing through her mind. The animal. That monster-dog, whatever it was, had attacked the man in the alley. The same man who'd tried to kill her. Roger! That *thing* had eaten him. That same beast she'd dreamed about her entire childhood.

"Oh my God! Oh my God! Oh my God!" She tried sucking in air but her lungs refused to work. The bright morning began to mute and fade from her awareness.

Please don't let me faint.

She felt herself being lifted off the ground and carried inside. In any other situation this would have been a dream come true, but all she wanted was to catch her breath.

"It'll be all right. You're safe now."

The enduring huskiness of his voice shifted through her awareness and weaved its way through the horror threatening to consume her. Her muscles relaxed, and that void she was about to fall into closed. Soon the memories stopped too. Peace transcended through her system. She drew a shuddery breath and clung to him.

Damn. He smells like melted chocolate. And why is he so warm?

When he eased her down to the couch, she refused to let go. Touching him was real. Hell, he was better than reality. Somehow he managed to stop the world from crashing in around her. She sensed that if she let go, she'd collapse completely. Still, she was no candy-ass dame who whimpered if she broke a nail. If she had to cling to him for a few minutes more, so be it. She'd get her shit together, just not this instant.

Why had tow-truck guy been in the alley in the first place? She definitely remembered him now. He'd saved her. And why had someone tried to kill her? And not just someone, but the witness, Roger Simmons?

Nothing made sense.

"That...that *thing* in the alley. You saw it. I know you did. What was it? An alien? A werewolf?" Her words muffled against the flesh of his chest. His hot, soft, chocolaty-smelling chest.

"Now you're being ridiculous."

His condescending tone cleaved through the mess of her brain and brought her back to the surface of lucidity. She pushed him away. "Why were you in the alley? I saw you."

He took a step back and gave a low growl.

Whether it was because of fear, anger, or frustration at being caught, she couldn't tell...but every hair on her neck stood at attention at the sound he made. She felt like a speck of dust in his presence. And for God's sake, why didn't he put a shirt on? Well, enough of this crap. She needed answers, not questions. And damn it, she was going to get them.

Before she could open her mouth, he asked, "What do you remember? Close your eyes and retrace your steps."

The rumbling baritone of his voice hummed through her like electricity and the power to do as he'd asked overrode everything.

She took a deep breath and filed through every vile detail before beginning. "The witness I came to Rio Morden to interview? He called me to meet him at Daly's Diner."

"A bit late for a meeting, don't you think?"

"Exactly what I said, but he told me it was important. He said it was something he needed to tell me. It's a small town, so I thought I'd be safe. I didn't expect to get, get..." She pinched her eyes tighter together.

"What happened next?"

"I left to meet him."

"Was someone at the front desk?"

Hannah shook her head. "No. I walked out of the motel and I remember the street was deserted. It was eerie."

"Were the lights on?"

She nodded. "Funny you mention that. They were dim, as if someone had turned them down or replaced all the bulbs with only 50-watt halogens. I thought that's just the way the town's lights were. After I was about halfway down the back lane, I was grabbed from behind."

The memory of those fingers that had tried to constrict the life out of her returned. She shuddered and wrapped her arms around herself, wishing tow-truck guy would do this for her instead.

"Keep your eyes closed. It'll help you remember. What did you smell?"

"At first, alcohol. It was on Roger's breath. He was scared; panting."

She lifted her head and stared right at him. "You're going to think I'm nuts, but what I'm about to tell you is the truth. I swear on a stack of Bibles. There was this...this, *sulfuric* smell. It burned my nose and made my eyes water. That thing, that animal, whatever it was, the stench came from it. The thing was huge and...and..."

She stopped with a quivering breath. "It began... Jesus, it started *eating* Roger. Holy crap! That's what it was doing. It was munching down on him like there was no tomorrow. Then I saw you."

"What do you think it was that you saw?"

Well, at least he didn't sound like he was going to have her committed to a padded room. In fact, he sounded curious to hear what she had to say. On top of that, he hadn't flinched or looked shocked when he saw her eyes. Now that was a first.

She didn't know why, but she felt compelled to tell the truth; that he'd know if she didn't. Maybe if she came clean, he would too.

She grasped her hands together and rushed the words out of her mouth. "You already blew my werewolf theory away, but to be honest..." She hesitated. "I've seen that monster before. Lots of times. I used to... Well, I still do, have these bouts of insomnia. Not as bad as when I was kid, thank goodness, but back then, when I finally went to sleep, I'd have these nightmares. That beast was always in them."

"Always?"

She nodded. "My nightmares are usually horrific. It's strange, though. Whenever I dreamt about him, it was like he knew I was there and tried to hide whatever it was he was doing, like he didn't want me to see. The same monster." She shuddered again. "He didn't do that last night."

Tow-truck guy just stood there listening.

Why isn't he laughing at me and calling it nonsense, like Mom used to do?

Neither of them said a word.

He studied her.

She scrutinized him back. Again, she felt a calming, protective cloud settle over her.

"Would you care for some breakfast?"

Whatever spell he'd charmed her with was immediately severed. Her cheeks flared with heat. "Are you insane? You want to go out and eat after what I just told you?"

"There's a restaurant..."

Fear raced like a disease through her, and it must have shown on her face.

"No, no. Not in Rio Morden," he added quickly. "There's a place about fifteen miles before the town of North Bend." He paused and glanced sheepishly around the room. "Housekeeping isn't high on my to-do list, as you can tell. And just so you know, I didn't kidnap you—or anything else."

He smiled, and she became a puddle of sweat.

Those teeth must have cost him a fortune. No wonder he lives like this. All his collateral is tied up in his mouth. Rational thought finally returned. "Where's my car?"

He tilted his head toward the gas pump outside.

She rose, wanting to be done with this business. She'd shared a part of herself that only her mother and the many shrinks she'd seen throughout her childhood knew about. "Thank you and all, but I have to get home and make a police report, and I need to tell my boss what happened. This is going to blow our case to shit."

She stopped and began gnawing the corner of her lip. Somehow, this was going to turn out to be all her fault. Could she end up being a potential witness? Gads! Then there'd be a conflict of interest. A possible mistrial? Could she lose her job? Wait a minute. How was she going to explain what really happened?

"I only asked you out for breakfast. Not to oath your firstborn to me."

"Excuse me?"

"You look like you're about to throw up."

"I was thinking about the case."

The corner of his mouth curled downward. "You a lawyer?"

Something told her he already knew she wasn't. Hanna shook her head in what she hoped was a nonchalant way and inched toward the door. The guy was creeping her out big time now. What sucked the most was she was attracted to him like a bitch in serious heat.

At this angle, his eyes caught the light coming in from the kitchen window. Red specks glinted back. But it was more than just their color. There was something she saw in them. Something intense. Something familiar. And whenever he looked at her – like he was doing now – she felt like he really *looked* at her.

She was a dowdy paralegal with fucked-up colored eyes and a bad case of sleepless nights. He was a knight in shining armor. Well, tattered armor, anyway. He was the rescuer, and she the idiot damsel in distress. To add insult to injury, she couldn't feel more like a loser if she tried.

"I'd gone to the motel to drop your car off last night. That's why I was in the alley."

Time stopped. A fly buzzed by her nose. Sweat tickled a path down the nape of her neck. If a speck of dust dropped, it would have sounded like a blaring trumpet.

"Would you do me the honor of having breakfast with me?"

"Pardon?" was all she could muster. She noted that his manner of speech sometimes sounded like a merry-go-round of eras.

"I'll drive you to the city myself and stand witness, if need be," he added.

Is this guy for real? She took another inch toward the front door. "You don't say? And just what am I supposed to tell the police? Or my boss? I need to speak with a lawyer, is what I have to do. Get some independent legal advice. Then a shrink. Yep, definitely a shrink." She took another step backward.

"Why did that man want to kill you?"

She stopped dead. She'd been asking herself the same question. "I don't know. I was supposed to take his statement, and that was it. Not get into an accident with you, and certainly not get myself killed, and..."

"And?" he pressed.

"Nothing," she mumbled. Her cheeks flared as hot as a fourth of July firework. *And not meet the hottest guy on the planet that makes my heart beat like a bongo drum.* What was she supposed to do now?

"Some people tend to think better on a full stomach. If you'll break your fast with me, I'd be honored. Maybe I can help."

There he went again with his strange vocabulary. At this point, what choice did she have? He'd helped her once already, and she desperately needed it. She nodded reluctantly. "Fine, but I'm driving my car."

"Let me find a clean shirt."

She watched him disappear around the hallway. His ass in those sweats was definitely something to write home about.

Damn it! She still hadn't asked him his name.

Chapter Seven

Rhune studied Hanna from the corner of his eye as she drove. Whenever she scrunched her forehead to see into the distance – like she was doing now – it created the loveliest creases between her eyes.

Those eyes.

She transfixed him; fascinated him. He could stare at her face all day and never tire of her. Her scent was a mixture of sweet 1625 brandy and early morning dew on freshly cut grass; so poignant that he wanted to roll himself all over her and keep her close forever.

She hadn't said a word since they'd left the garage, but the stiffness of her body spoke volumes.

Uncertainty coiled in the pit of his stomach.

Her eyes.

He'd seen them time and time before—but their intensity then wasn't like it was now.

Through the mutilated flesh and fountains of blood, he'd sensed those eyes watching him, always filled with fear, always traumatized and swimming with tears. Their colors had struck him dumb each and every time they focused on him. They reached for him, touched him, and quelled the viciousness of his beast. An unquenchable need to protect her had always followed. Now, in living flesh, that hadn't changed in the least. He now knew for certain what she was.

Does she know? he wondered. Unease parked itself deep inside and took residence.

He pushed aside his misgivings and gave her directions to the outskirts of North Bend. Soon a parking lot lined with eighteen wheelers darkened the horizon.

After she parked, he jumped out and rushed to the driver's side to hold open her door. Easing his hand into the small of her back, he guided her inside to a booth by a window overlooking the highway. She said nothing as she walked stiff-legged to their table.

Some restaurant patrons shifted in their chairs but paid them no more attention before returning to their plates of food.

He waited for her to sit first, then he slid into the booth across from her. As soon as his rear made contact with his seat, a sudden rush of *something* sent ice down his spine, but it disappeared before he could figure out what it was, and why.

She peered out the window, her complexion pale, and her features haggard from sleep deprivation, which darkened the delicate skin beneath both her remarkable eyes.

Placing his elbows on the table, he pushed forward slightly, but still far enough away as to not invade her personal space. She was a frightened deer looking down the barrel of a gun. And he was that weapon. She was either going to fight, or flee. He prayed for the latter.

"Tell me what you think you saw," he asked softly.

She turned to him. "Who are you? I mean, what's your name?"

"Rhune. With an 'h.' And you?"

"Hanna. Hanna Carmichael. What's your last name?"

"It's just Rhune."

"Like Prince?"

"I was. A long time ago."

Her face etched with puzzlement.

"What case are you working on?"

"The Drysdale murder."

"Adam Drysdale? The famous lawyer?"

"You've read about it? Roger's deposition was vital to our case."

"Perhaps the two are connected?"

"Then explain to me why some mutant Fido is out there right now digesting him."

He flinched at her description and chose his next words carefully. "Maybe it was time to pay the piper for his sins?"

"That'll read great on a police report," she snapped.

He pushed back into the booth and crossed his arms. "Do you believe in the afterlife?"

"What does that have to do with anything?"

"Everything."

She leaned back like him. "I believe there are places we go after we die."

"How do you think we get there?"

"Some follow a white light. Some fall into flames. I don't know. I've never died before." She puffed out a sigh.

"How do you think souls travel to their final destinations?" He sensed the wheels turning in her head.

"To be honest, I've never given it much thought."

There were rules against sharing what he was privy to, and he'd never broken one before. So why did he harbor such a compulsion to do so now? *I have to make her understand, that's why.*

He took a deep breath and began. "What if I told you that some people can walk between the veils of light and dark, often in dreams, like you?"

"Me?"

"You know how some people can read other people's thoughts? Or move objects with their minds?"

She nodded, albeit skeptically.

"Those people have extraordinary skills. They use parts of their brain that usually lie dormant in most. Depending on how they use them, they've been touched by either the hand of God—or Asmodeus, the devil. There's a reason why they're chosen."

Her one eyebrow inched up. "Really? What does this have to do with last night?"

"You said you've seen that animal before in your dreams, correct? Perhaps you were peering through the veils."

She threw up her hands. "What veils?"

The customer closest to them lifted his head, his lips shiny from a strip of bacon dangling between them. When Rhune shot him a glare, he was quick to dig back into his eggs with a corner of his toast, more intent on consuming his meal than on eavesdropping.

He lowered his voice. "What do you believe, Hanna?"

Pursing her lips, she glanced out the window again. "I don't know. I thought you just got sucked into the earth or something."

He waited patiently until she looked his way again. Then he asked, "What if that thing you saw was delivering Roger to Hell?"

"Like a, a...?"

He nodded, watching her every reaction.

She leaned closer to the table and hissed, "A hellhound? Are you certifiably insane?"

"No."

"You're telling me that..." She stopped and shook her head. "I'm not going to repeat it."

He tried another approach. "Why was that creature you saw the same as in your dreams?"

"Because I was a kid, damn it! Kids dream about monsters."

This time two different heads swiveled their way. Maybe it hadn't been such a good idea coming here. He'd hoped if she were in a normal setting she'd feel more comfortable. Safer.

He lowered his voice to a whisper. "What if I were to tell you that hellhounds are real? That they deliver souls to Hell? That they work for God, contrary to popular folklore. And some people can see them in dreams, like you."

Her cheeks paled to the color of milk. "Bullshit."

The waitress happened to pick that inopportune time to stop at their table. "What'll you two be having?" she asked in between the snapping of her gum.

When he forced a smile her way, a flush of pink stained the woman's leathery cheeks. Yeah, he had a way with women, but apparently, not with the one sitting across from him. "Give us a few minutes more, please?"

The waitress grinned and batted her false eyelashes. "Sure thing, sugar. Just give me a holler. I'll be right over there by the counter." She strolled away with several backward glances.

Hanna hadn't noticed, as she'd turned her attention out the window again.

"What if you have the ability to see, and even travel, between these veils?" *Let's hope that's all she can do.*

She turned to him with a unwavering stare. "All I know is that I don't know what I saw, but I have to explain it to my boss. And the authorities. Your theory doesn't cut it in the real world. Can you see their faces when I tell them, 'Oh, not to worry, Mr. Police Officer. Roger tried to kill me, but a big, bad hellhound showed up and ate him. Now he's where he belongs. But wait. When, and if, I sleep tonight, I'll drop by and ask him all about it.'"

Her sarcasm was thick enough to cut with a chainsaw. But Rhune had a plan already formulating. "What if you don't have to?"

Those stunning eyes of hers narrowed. "What do you mean?" Hannah asked testily.

"You go back to the city and say nothing."

"What?"

"No one knows you went to meet Roger, right?"

"Yes, but—"

"After you took his statement, you went and checked into your hotel, and then left to grab a bite to eat, but everything was closed."

"Daly's Diner is open all night, or so Roger told me."

"No, it's not. He lied to get you in the alley. When you returned, no one was at the front desk, so you left. At that moment, I happened to come by to drop off your car. I drove you back to my place." The more he thought about, the more he knew it would work.

Judging by the scowling skepticism darkening every line on her face, he still needed to convince her. "People saw us together yesterday, including Ben Hardy. You could say I asked you out for dinner and—"

"You think pretty highly of yourself, don't you?"

He gave a sheepish shrug.

She scowled back. "And just how stupid does that make me look?"

She had a point. "How about I wooed you off your feet?"

Her face turned fiery red. She opened her mouth, but nothing came out.

"Look," he continued. "We return to Rio Morden after breakfast and grab your bag. We trash your room and head straight to the Sheriff's office and tell them your room was vandalized. All you'll be doing is reporting a break-in. With Roger missing, they might assume it'd been him and he took off out of town afterward."

She was quiet for so long, he feared she'd get up and walk out. *Where would she go?*

"Okay, *just* Rhune. I can believe that, but what happens when Roger is called to testify? What am I supposed to do then? What do I tell my boss?" Hysteria edged into her words.

"No one knows about his phone call to you. You met with him yesterday afternoon, took his statement, went to your hotel, and that's the last you saw of him. Even if they trace the phone records, they'll know he called you at the hotel, but you weren't there. Believe me. No one's going to find him."

"But that's lying! Wait. How do you know no one's going to find him? Forensics—"

"There's nothing to find. Not a drop of blood. Not a splinter of bone. He never existed. Would you rather explain what really happened?"

"But I don't know what happened! Holy shit! My briefcase!"

This time, every head in the restaurant turned toward them. Tears brimmed in her eyes before she wiped them away with an angry swipe.

He inched his hand across the table and took one of hers. Through his touch, he injected Hannah with a sliver of his magic.

Her head jerked up. Her eyes widened. She immediately pulled away as if he'd singed her.

"How did you do that?"

He smiled. "It's a gift."

"Are you always, um, this warm?" Her face was now fire hydrant red.

He didn't answer.

"We have to find my briefcase. I dropped it in the alley."

"Then we'll go there first and retrieve it."

"This changes everything. You know that, right? I'm trusting a man I've just met. I've been a witness to a murder that I can't tell anyone about. And even if I did, who'd friggin' believe me? I'm a horrible liar. I won't be able to pull this off. I can't. Jesus, what am I going to do?"

"I'll help."

Hanna leaned into the cushions of the booth and studied him for the longest time. "Why are you doing this? You don't even know me."

"I believe you, Hanna. You shouldn't have seen what you did."

Her brow arched. "Really?"

He knew he was stretching the limits of his oath, but he couldn't help himself. "Yes, because I've seen them too."

Chapter Eight

Their breakfast had been brief. Hanna managed a couple of sips of some lukewarm tea and a half-piece of dry toast. Rhune had ordered the He-Man breakfast, but barely touched his plate.

Still reeling from their little pow-wow session, she allowed him to drive her car back to Rio Morden while she focused on the scenery whizzing by the window.

Staring at him was like being sucked into a deep, dark hole. She'd become Alice in Wonderland, except she'd landed in Hell. And like Alice, she wanted nothing more than to jump into that hole and find out where it led.

Man, was she screwed up.

What they were about to do was against the law. She knew it. Rhune knew it. Probably half the restaurant knew it too, but she was still going to do it. What other choice did she have? How had her little, boring world exploded into absolute mayhem?

Meeting tow-truck guy, that's how.

With each passing mile back to town, her stomach muscles tightened. Anxiety skyrocketed. Fear filled her to the core.

Please, please, please, don't let me up-chuck on the front seat. The car rental place will never let me use one of their cars again. She swallowed hard and tried to make light conversation.

After they'd commented on the weather four times, she gave up making small talk. Instead, she found herself staring at his fingers on the steering wheel, then following the deep, rippling outline of muscles on his forearms. His thigh was close. Too close.

The heat radiating off him made her want to move closer and wrap herself around him. She felt safe in his presence. And the way he smelled of something sweet melting in a pot.

Geeze Louise. She'd never seen a man as ruggedly handsome as him, and that was one of the reasons she found it so difficult to look at him without becoming a puddle in her seat. He was trying to help her. A stranger. Why? The gentleness she sensed in him was so attractive, yet he also seemed fierce, like some ancient warrior. He made her feel protected and warm. Very warm.

Better yet, he appeared interested in her. That was something new. Most men didn't give her a second look, and certainly not ones that looked anything like him. Sadly, she usually became a blubbering idiot in front of hot guys. Why not now?

She gave herself a stern shake. *This is ridiculous! Just look out the window. You're not going to be dating him any time soon, for goodness sake.*

When they turned off I-18 and started down Rio Morden's main street, they stopped first in the alley. Her briefcase was exactly where she thought she'd dropped it. And just as Rhune had said, there was nothing evidencing that someone had been ripped apart limb by limb and devoured. She got back into the car, her body shaking with dread.

Rhune then did something that set her heart hammering wildly out of control. The timid touch of his fingers on her arm brought a rush of well-being, strength, and incredible warmth that settled every raging nerve in her body. It was pure magic. How he did that little trick was beyond her scope of understanding, but she was thankful for it. She forced a half-ass smile his way and braced herself for what was coming next.

By the time they'd parked in front of The Mercury Inn, she felt she had the courage to go through with the charade. She got out of the truck and stepped onto the sidewalk. His right hand landed softly into the hollow of her back as he guided her forward like he was some English lord. He was definitely old-fashioned with his manners. Just another trait of his that she found attractive.

They found Mrs. Grady in high panic mode. Strands of her wiry, gray hair had escaped the tight bun at the back of her head and flapped about her sweaty face as she apologized to the high heavens for the break-in. Hanna murmured something intangible and left Rhune to deal with her.

Stepping over splintered parts of the doorframe of her room, Hanna stared about at the mess the intruder left behind, totally confused as to why someone would break into *her* room. At least they didn't have to fabricate that part of their story. *How convenient.*

She grabbed her one bag and stopped long enough to tell the squawking woman she was heading to the Sheriff's office to file a report. When she tried to pay, the woman waved away her money.

"The room's been taken care of," she said, giving a nervous smile in Rhune's direction.

Two hours later, they were back on I-18.

"How convenient was it that my room was broken into?"

"Wasn't it though?" Rhune murmured thoughtfully.

"This is insane."

"Yes, it is, but I think it went well. Don't you?"

"Which part?" Hanna asked wearily. She felt as if she'd been washed and ironed several times over.

"The Sheriff believed you."

"Really?" She rolled her eyes and picked nervously at the strap of her overnight bag.

"Absolutely."

The conviction in his tone weirded her out. She didn't feel like talking, so she rolled down the window to let the wind blow through whatever brain cells she had left, which weren't many. Guilt rolled through her like molten lead.

She'd lied to a Sheriff. An officer of the law. Wasn't she supposed to be a representative of the justice system? She could go to jail for what she'd just done. If she'd told the truth, however, she'd be dosed up on a hundred cc's of Lorazepam and plopped into a hospital with those fancy bars on the windows for the rest of her life. She'd seen enough doctors in her day because of those damn dreams of hers, and it would be a rainy day in the Sahara before she'd suffer through that again.

But she hadn't really lied. Her room *had* been broken into. *Why?*

Rhune believes me. He's seen those monster-dogs too. She stole a sidelong glance in his direction.

There was a tranquility about him; a stillness she found both comforting and confusing. And there was something else. Something dangerous and ethereal. He reminded her of her late father. Mild and meek, until pissed off. Then watch out.

"You can leave as soon as we get back to the gas station."

"Thanks." Knowing that she had to face Mr. Winford and go through this farce again—alone— brought a bubble of bile to sour her tongue.

A gleam of metal caught in the rearview mirror for mere seconds before the sports car whizzed by Rhune's open window doing over a hundred miles an hour. He frowned. "That idiot's going to kill someone."

She cupped her chin in her hand and watched the fields go by, worrying about what she'd say to her boss rather than some kid speeding in daddy's car.

A cloud of dust rose around them as they pulled into the rutted lot of his gas station. She went to get out, but he was at her door before she had the handle pulled. *What is with him and that eloquent attitude? And his vocabulary?*

"You have at least a four-hour drive back to the city. If you leave now, you should have only about a half hour of night driving. Then you'll be in the city limits."

She wasn't going to admit it, but she was scared to death. Scant comfort came knowing that as long as she didn't sleep, she'd be okay. If she dreamed of that beast again, she'd be alone and shit out of luck. Tow-truck guy wouldn't be there to save her. The thought made her actually puke a little in her mouth.

"You have to leave. Now."

"Are you trying to get rid of me?" she managed past the curdled spit.

"No. I just want you to get home safe."

"I need your phone number. I can't make it out on the card you gave me."

He tilted his head while a small smile played at the corners of his mouth.

Crap! That sounded lame. "What I mean is if I have to get a hold of you to...you know, collaborate my story."

"I'll try and find another business card for you. I would very much enjoy talking to you again."

One minute 21st century. The next, he time-warped backward.

Rhune turned and headed inside. She gave a long look at his ass and memorized it. She wouldn't be seeing one like it for a very long time, if ever. His strides were long and precise; his t-shirt clinging to every muscle at all the right angles. *A dancer's body, but with bulkier muscles,* she mused wistfully.

After he disappeared inside, she opened her car door, tossed in her purse and briefcase, and pulled the trunk latch. When she made for the handle of her overnight bag, Rhune was suddenly there taking it from her hand and placing it into the vehicle.

She jumped with a squeak. "Jesus! Stop doing that."

He frowned. "You know, swearing doesn't become you."

She should have heard gravel crunching underfoot as he approached, but there'd been nothing. Something about the guy was beyond spooky. Delicious, but still spooky, and so right to look at.

Hanna hurried toward the open car door. "I have to go." There was something definitely odd about him. No doubt about it, and she had several hours to think and categorically file it away forever. She was a paralegal, for Christ's sake. Somehow, somewhere, she'd find a logical answer.

Holding out another business card, he took a step toward her. On impulse, she skittered back.

"Are you sure you're all right?"

Is that regret in his eyes? Don't be an idiot. He's glad to see me go. She grabbed the card and stuffed it into her purse. "I have to... Um, thank you. For everything." *Oh my God, you lame-o!*

She slammed the car door shut, pushed the key into the ignition, and peeled out of the yard. As she drove the straight line down I-18 towards the city, her insides squirmed like a thousand worms had checked in for a holiday. Nothing in her world felt real anymore, and the thought was absolutely terrifying.

The cramps in her knuckles from gripping the steering wheel lessened with each mile Hanna put behind her. She began feeling a bit normal, until...

Rhune was suddenly standing in front of her car as a ghostly apparition, just like he had looked in the alley. She should have been driving through him, but she wasn't.

His voice reached through her shock and demanded she listen. *"Don't stop until you get to the city. Not even for the police. Escape at all cost."*

She immediately went for the brake.

"No. Don't stop."

This was one hallucination she couldn't ignore. Every fiber of her being told her to do as he said.

"Go faster." Then he vanished into billowing smoke.

"I've landed in the fucking Twilight Zone." With her foot still hovering over the brake, she realized she couldn't bring herself to press down on it. Something in Rhune's imaginary voice scared her to death. Danger nipped in the air around her.

In her mind's eye, she saw him jump onto a rustic red and white Harley and drive after her. She put the cruise control on eighty and stared straight ahead, praying there were no speed traps—and that Rhune would catch up to her.

Chapter Nine

Hanna made it home without incident, although it had started to rain about twenty miles from the Perimeter, which was the main highway that wound around the city limits.

She drove carefully through the slick covered streets and dropped off the rental car. After it passed a glowing inspection, she waved down a cab. Sitting in the back, she peered out every window, especially the one behind her. No one seemed to be following. Then again, how would she know?

She paid the cabbie, asked for a receipt for the office's accountant, and bee-lined it into her apartment. Slamming the deadbolt into place didn't cut it. With her nerves stretched beyond their limits, the feeling of being watched wouldn't go away, even after pushing her desk up against the apartment's door.

She gazed about her small suite. Everything looked as she'd left it. Living on the fifth floor didn't feel so bad now. She made a mental note to remember this moment on those days the elevator didn't work, which was every other week.

Since suffering that hallucination of Rhune on the highway, she had teetered on a thin edge of sanity. She dropped her apartment keys on the small table by the front door and ventured into the kitchen. The blinking light on her answering machine caught her attention. She pressed play and proceeded to undress for a well-needed shower.

Just as she reached the bathroom door, she stopped dead in her tracks. The voice on the machine sounded drier than usual. "Hanna, call me the instant you get back."

Mr. Winford had never called her at home, however, he'd have to wait. She wasn't in the mood to talk to anyone—except Rhune.

Standing beneath sprays of hot water, she rehashed everything that had happened within the last twenty-four hours. It was as if Rhune had moved inside her head and was paying her rent to be there. Not that that was a bad thing, mind you, but the mitigating circumstances as to why he was there made her want to scream. The image of him standing by the pump with no shirt on and wearing those gray sweatpants kept giving her libido a kick she didn't need. Damn, he was the photoshopped perfection of the male species.

I've hallucinated everything. It happens when one doesn't get enough sleep. He's probably drinking a beer, watching that big-ass TV of his, and glad he's seen the last of me.

She reached for the shampoo and tried to think of something else, but question after question jounced through her skull. The more she kept thinking, the more her head hurt.

It took all her energy to dry herself off and get into a pair of clean pajamas. Exhausted both in mind and body, she popped a few aspirins and headed into the kitchen, her thoughts still running a mile a minute.

How could I dream up a man hovering in the air outside my windshield while driving seventy miles an hour? It hadn't been real, that's why. Just your overactive imagination again.

She shuddered. Now she sounded just like her mother.

She made a cup of honeyed tea, climbed into bed, and turned on the television.

One minute she was watching Conan, the next...

Shit! Not again!

She found herself on her hands and knees in the middle of a cobblestone road. If she didn't know better, she'd swear she'd been transported to merry ol' England, circa early 1800's. Everything was tinged dull sepia, except for the fog. It glowed like copper and clung to her with invisible fingers. Mist puffed out from between her lips, though the air felt thick and sauna-like. The silence sat on her shoulders like a heavy, breathing thing.

At first, it sounded like tree branches rubbing against one another in the wind, but not a hair moved on her head. Then it got louder, drawing closer. The ground beneath her began to *thump*.

Something approached.

Something big.

Something heavy.

With her heart pounding and her body shaking, Hanna frantically searched for a place to hide, but when she tried to get up and run, her body wouldn't move. It was as if she'd been glued to the center of the road.

The vibrations in the ground drew nearer.

Faster.

Pebbles bounced around her hands.

She squeezed her eyes shut. Tears leaked from the corners. *Wake up! Wake up, you idiot! WAKE UP.*

When heavy breathing sounded directly behind her, there was no way in hell she was opening her eyes and looking. No freaking way at all. If she were going to get eaten, she'd rather not see it.

Gravel crunched underfoot. Then it stopped. She heard sniffing. It took a few steps closer.

She tried to swallow, but every drop of spit had dried up. The boulder lodged in her throat wouldn't move. Her lungs cried for oxygen.

"You're not supposed to be here."

Hanna almost had an aneurysm. It spoke! That same sulfuric smell was back, harsher and stronger than in the alley. The dead air around her became several degrees hotter. Sweat dripped down her forehead and seeped into her eyes, making them sting and water more. Her nose burned. She took a chance and peeked. The color of the fog had changed to a reddish-brown.

Suddenly, the awful smell disappeared and Hanna's eyes stopped watering. Whatever power had been holding her to the flagstones let go and she bolted to her feet. Even though she wanted to run as fast as her legs could take her, something compelled her to turn and look up.

Way up.

There stood the demon-dog in all its gory glory, but this time, he looked—curious? Not the usual insane, hell-bent monster about to devour somebody. Eyes of flickering flames held intelligence instead of the gruesome madness she'd seen in the alley and in her dreams. There was something proverbial about them. They were the same eyes from her nightmares, yes, but...?

"You shouldn't be here. Leave Gehenna. Rouse yourself."

The voice reverberated inside her head like a trumpet blasting close to her ear. Without realizing, she lifted her hand to touch him.

The beast reared back. Shock shone in its eyes— eyes she'd seen before. *But from where?*

Without a word, the monster continued on its way down the center of the road and disappeared into the eerie mist.

She stood there with her mouth hanging open and an annoying sound ricocheting in her ears. It grew louder and more irritating, like a thousand bumblebees had made a nest inside her skull.

She blinked.

Pins and needles burned up and down the arm she'd fallen asleep on. Every blanket and pillow looked as if she'd done battle with them—and lost. Her glass of water on the nightstand had tipped over, leaving a small puddle on the carpet.

She then realized that the buzzing in her head was her alarm clock. She slammed her hand down on the 'off' button and stumbled out of bed. Her heart beat so fast, she almost swooned. Movement caught her eye.

Standing in the hallway by the bathroom door was Rhune. She gasped.

"Thank goodness, you're safe."

Stunned, she whirled in the direction of her front door, which she could see from her bedroom. The desk and deadbolt were exactly as she'd left them. Her heart began pounding way too fast. "How did you...?"

The rest of the words failed to pass her lips as she fainted away.

Chapter Ten

How was he going to explain that this was her fault? That he'd been caught in her dream and brought here by her. He'd heard this happening to other hounds with Dreamwalkers, but not that often. And never him.

How strong is she?

He'd sensed the danger the moment Hanna left the gas station. Homing in on her scent had been easy, but his bike hadn't been fast enough to catch her before she reached the city limits.

When his hellhound began battling to be free, Rhune had parked his Harley on the side of the road. With seconds to spare, he had placed a concealment spell over the motorcycle before the transformation took over and whisked him off to another plane of existence. He'd found his t'elan for the night, made the delivery without incident, until...

He'd found Hanna on all fours in the middle of Gehenna—the City of the Dead. That had never happened before either. Dreamwalkers were drawn to hellhounds because of the extreme emotions emanating from t'elans in the throes of their demise. How had he become inexplicably tied to one? And the same girl who'd haunted him for years with those amazing eyes?

Now he was picking her off the floor of her apartment, where he'd made her faint dead away for a second time. *How much more can this poor woman sustain?*

He lifted her into his arms and placed her on her messy bed. Uncertain what to do next, he snatched the overturned glass, went to the bathroom, refilled it, and returned.

When she finally opened her eyes, she gave a choked scream, grabbed her blanket and scuttled backward until her spine hit against the wall behind her bed. Her wild gaze darted from side-to-side, searching for an escape.

Not wanting to frighten her more than he already had, he stepped back and said nothing, feeling like a Grade-A jackass.

Suddenly the phone rang. Hanna's eyes rounded, but she made no move to get it.

When it continued ringing, he asked, "Aren't you going to get that?"

"N-No. This isn't real. You're not real. I'm still dreaming."

A machine beeped and from where he stood, Rhune heard a tinny voice recording a message. "Hanna? Hanna, are you there? Pick up, damn it. What the hell happened in Rio Morden? Where are you?"

"That's my boss," she whispered past trembling lips.

"So that's Lucifer's brother?"

Her eyes went wider. "I have a trial tomorrow. I need to get ready for, for work. My boss...?"

He'd made up his mind to tell her everything that he could. Unfortunately, this wasn't the time. But seriously? Was any time going to be right to tell her what he did for a living? And how much trouble was he going to get into for doing so?

Something else was at work here. Rhune felt it as deeply as he sensed Hanna's essence. "Might I stay here and wait for your return this evening?"

Her eyes widened even more, which made her unshed tears spill down her cheeks. This wasn't good. He could see he was driving her to the edge. Yet again, she surprised him.

"No you may not! And stop talking like that. How the heck did you get in here? Holy shit! Never mind. I can't think about this right now. You have to leave. Get out of my apartment. Now!"

She spared a glance at the clock on the night table. "And I'm late for work. Shit!"

"Hanna, you're in danger. I can't explain how I know, but I promise I'll tell you what I can this evening. You have to trust me."

He hoped she'd hear the sincerity and urgency in his voice. Someone was trying to kill her, that much he'd gleaned off the t'elan in the alley; however, someone else was pulling the strings. Whoever he or she was, he had a pretty good sense that it had to do with the case she was currently working on.

When he saw her hesitate, he almost sighed with relief.

She dropped the sheet and stormed to the front door. Grunting from the effort, she shoved the desk out of the way and fumbled with the locks before throwing the door wide open. She raised her arm and pointed out into the hallway. "Get out."

"Han—"

"I said get OUT." She cringed and peered next door for a moment.

Frustration bubbled and churned in his gut, but he understood her reluctance. If their roles had been reversed, he was damned sure he wouldn't be handling the situation half as well as she was doing. "I shall abide by your wishes, but I'm not leaving the city. I'll call on you tonight, and we can discuss this rationally."

He refused to stand by and do nothing. Hanna had gotten under his skin big time and no matter how many times he told himself to let it go, he couldn't.

Or was it because he didn't want to let her go?

When the door slammed behind him, he stood in the hallway for the longest time listening to the activity inside. He sniffed the air. Something didn't taste right. His senses as a human weren't usually this acute. She'd brought him here, so maybe that was the reason.

She doesn't know the power she possesses.

He left her apartment and headed to a restaurant he'd seen across the street. The five-and-dime diner had a vacant table by the window which gave a direct line of sight to her building. When the waitress approached to take his order, he asked for a cup of coffee. As she was about to walk away, he added, "Bring a couple pots."

Chapter Eleven

Hanna snagged the zipper of her skirt into the fabric of her panties three times before getting it done up properly. If she ended up in an accident before making it to the office, so be it… Wearing ripped underwear was the least of her worries. It took forever to fumble with the buttons of her blouse because her hands wouldn't stop shaking.

How had Rhune managed to get into her apartment? He'd suddenly appeared in the alley. Then outside her windshield. Now this? Her world had turned into a cheap magic show, and tow-truck guy was completely to blame.

She picked up her briefcase, shot a fleeting glance around the kitchen, then stopped. *But if I hadn't met him, I'd most likely be dead. Hell! Gads! Stop saying that word, you idiot! This isn't Hell. You're going to work. You tell your story, say you're sick, and go home. Winford will do the trial and everything will go back to normal. Roger flew the coop. He got cold feet at the thought of having to testify and took off. If Winford asks, that's all I have to say.*

After grabbing a week-old bagel she could have used as a paperweight, she was out the door. She checked her watch and groaned. Even if she took a cab, she'd be at least thirty minutes late—again—and about twenty bucks poorer. Counting last night's fare home, she was running short on funds. The first thing she was going to do when she got to the office was to get reimbursed. Then she'd talk to Winford.

She raised her arm and flagged down a cab.

As the city streets went by, she tried to concentrate on the trial. The thought of speaking with Mr. Winford made the bagel she'd wolfed down solidify like a brick in her stomach. Would she be able to pull this off without Rhune's help? Well, she had about five minutes to find out.

Staring out the cab's window, she thought about Roger and the events that had followed since her trip to Rio Morden. One detail ran into another. Even her best analytical skills couldn't sort out what was real and what wasn't...except Rhune. He was real.

Her head pounded, and it was only eight forty-five in the morning.

"Where's Simmons?"

Careful to keep her gaze averted, Hanna handed Winford the signed statement from her briefcase, hoping he didn't notice the shaking of her hands. "I don't know."

"What do you mean 'you don't know?'" he asked coldly.

"I met with him. Took his deposition, and that was it."

"Nothing else happened?"

"Well, my room at the motel was vandalized. I had to make a police report."

He gave the paper a cursory glance before tossing it on his desk without a second look. "I've been trying to reach Simmons all morning. He's not answering his cell."

She shrugged and studied the family picture on his desk. "Maybe he got cold feet?"

"Without him taking the stand to support his evidence, we have nothing!"

She flinched at the anger in his voice. This trial was getting to him. *He's not the only one,* she thought. "We have a signed statement. We can rely on that," she added meekly.

"It'll mean diddly-squat when the defendant's counsel demands to cross-examine him on it." He took a deep breath. "Look, I'm not mad at you. He's vital to our case. We need to find him. Fast."

"I know that, but I have no idea where he is. I went to Rio Morden as you asked. Got his statement, and I came home. Maybe we can ask for a continuance—"

He growled. "How do you think that's going to look?"

Just as she suspected, this was turning out to be her fault. "He's not going to be called today, probably not even by Friday. The defense has to put forth their evidence first."

"Thanks for the news flash, Hanna. I know how a trial operates. We're submitting his statement today. Once Andrews' defense team reads it, they're going to want to call Simmons as soon as possible. We're taking no chances on losing this one. Now find him."

Mr. Winford turned in his chair. The dismissal was rude and totally uncalled for.

She stood slowly, nursing her anger and frustration. "I went out of my way to travel to Rio Morden to get that statement for you. I don't deserve to be treated like this. And it's not my job to find someone."

The instant the words left her mouth, she instantly regretted them. In fact, she'd never spoken to him like that before, but damn it, he pissed her off.

Winford's chair squeaked as he shifted back around. His beady eyes narrowed, and his lips pursed until they were purple.

"W-What I meant to say is, why do I have to look for him? We have private investigators on staff for that."

His tone was so cold she swore she saw mist come from his mouth. "Because *you* were the last one who saw him, that's why. If he's hiding, I'm sure you'll be able to coax him out."

Her moment of bravado flickered and winked out like a birthday candle caught in a hurricane. "How am I to get back to Rio Morden?"

He dug into a drawer of his desk, pulled out a credit card and tossed it in her direction. "That's the office's VISA. Rent one. Keep every receipt and give them only to me when you get back. We're delivering preliminaries before the judge this morning, so that'll buy us some time. I'll give you a day before I submit his statement. Find Roger Simmons. Got it?"

Refusing to trust her voice, she merely nodded, grabbed the credit card, and rushed out of his office. With her heart hammering inside of her chest, she managed to make it to her desk without passing out.

She'd pulled off the lie—barely—and without Rhune's help. Then reality kicked in. *How do I find a guy who's been eaten by a monster?*

She needed tow-truck guy more than she cared to admit.

———◆———

The man standing by the front door of Hanna's apartment block sparked more than Rhune's curiosity. Or perhaps it was the six hours spent in utter boredom with almost two pots of coffee eating away the lining of his innards.

He got up and was in the process of leaving some money on the table when he saw the stranger slink inside just after a tenant had left.

Something about the guy felt wrong. Rhune placed a ten dollar bill on the table and left the restaurant without waiting for his change.

As he jogged across the street, the heat of someone's stare drilled into his back. When he stopped at the apartment's entrance, he looked down one end of the street and then the other. No one appeared overly curious or stood out as suspicious. Rhune shook his head and worked the security door open, thankful his magic had some practical uses in this age. He hurried inside.

The late 1970's ten-story brick building had narrow hallways and musty-smelling carpets. Although there were two elevators on his left, Rhune raced up the stairwell to the fifth floor and opened the emergency exit door a crack.

From his vantage point, the man he'd seen outside stood in front of Hanna's apartment door. With his hoodie pulled low over his head, Rhune couldn't see his face.

The man looked one way and then the other before fidgeting with her lock. A muted *click* resonated down the hallway. Soundlessly, the intruder stepped inside and closed the door behind him.

Fury rolled through Rhune. If that man harmed one hair on Hanna's head, he'd rip him limb from limb. He tempered the beast inside before stepping out from the stairwell and heading for Hanna's door. He turned the knob. The idiot hadn't bothered to relock it. Rhune stepped quietly inside.

The faint sounds of drawers being opened and closed came from Hanna's bedroom. Then a rustling of papers. He backed up against the wall in the kitchen just as the stranger lumbered out of her bedroom and into the hall.

The man's scent chased through Rhune's nose. He'd smelled it earlier. The guy had been in Hanna's apartment building before. He sucked in a breath and stepped out into the open.

In a flash, the intruder drew a knife and brandished the blade in front of him. "What the fuck are you doing in here?"

"I might ask you the same question," he said more calmly than he felt.

The man's gaze flitted left to right. He was cornered. Rhune knew it, and he knew it. That made him all the more dangerous.

"This is my apartment. Get the hell out of here. I'm calling the police."

"I'll dial 911 for you."

A dangerous mask slipped over the stranger's face.

As Rhune suspected, he came running at him full tilt. The impact knocked him back into the wall. Faster than he thought possible, the man was out the door.

Rhune took off after him. Down the hall, he heard the stairwell door bang open. He followed.

Seconds later the sound of footfalls on the stairs faded. By the time Rhune reached the front door and was standing outside, the guy had vanished.

He did a slow turn and sniffed at the air. There were too many scents that conflicted with the lingering stink of the stranger. There was no way he could trail him.

Something dangerous was going on, and damn it, he was going to put a stop to it. More importantly, he needed to ensure Hanna was safe. The determination—no—the *need* to do so was as odd to him as being in this claustrophobic city. Unfortunately, he'd have to find shelter before nightfall, and nowhere near Hanna's apartment. He couldn't allow his beast to be near her, especially now when someone else had the power to gain control over him.

But he knew that no matter how many miles he put between himself and her, the beast inside would find her.

Chapter Twelve

With money in her pocket from being reimbursed for her out-of-pocket expenses, Hanna walked home instead. She dragged her feet all the way, trying to think of a solution. There was no way Roger was ever going to take the stand...unless he showed up as a ghost. And with all the wacky things that had happened so far, that wouldn't have surprised her in the least.

About eight blocks from her apartment, it began to pour. She stopped on the sidewalk and glared up at the sky. "You just don't like me, do you?"

By the time she reached the front door of her apartment, even her panties were soaked, and not in a good way. She fumbled with the lock and discovered the deadbolt wasn't in place. She froze. She swore she'd locked the door before leaving for work. Then again, her mind had been racing in a hundred different directions she probably forgot.

With a sigh, she entered her apartment, clicked the deadbolt into place—and screamed.

Rhune stood in the hallway, his arms crossed, and his face like death. Those tiny red specks glowed in his eyes. "You're safe."

Before she could scream again, he took her into his arms and crushed her against his chest. He held her so tightly, the blood in her head pounded in conjunction with her heartbeat. "I 'en't breaze," she managed to say.

He let go and stumbled a few feet back. "I apologize for my forwardness."

She instantly wished he hadn't moved away. For those scant seconds, she felt safe and warm.

His cheeks flushed as he bounced from foot to foot. "I, um... I'm sorry."

Between wanting to yell at him for almost scaring her to death and wishing she could fall into his arms again, frantic knocking sounded outside the door.

"Hanna? Hanna? Are you all right, dear?"

Mrs. Tierney from next door did another frantic round of knocking. "Hanna? Are you in there? I'm calling the police if you don't answer right now!"

Hanna rolled her eyes and placed a finger against her lips before turning and opening the door. "Yes, Mrs. Tierney. I'm home. I tripped over a shoe, is all. Stubbed my toe."

"Are you sure? I heard you were upset with someone this morning."

Rhune went rigid. He shook his head, his gaze shooting from the door to her, begging her not to say anything.

"I'm okay."

"And there was a commotion in the hallway earlier today. When I went out to check, I saw a man leaving through the fire escape. A stranger in the hallway is always trouble. And they call this a secure building. As long as I know you're all right. Good night, dear."

Hanna scrunched up her face and scowled at the man who'd caused all of this. "Thank you, Mrs. Tierney. My, um, brother had come for a visit. I gave him my key. That was probably him you saw. He was late to catch his flight home, as usual. Thanks again for the neighborhood watch."

When she heard the neighbor's door close, she whirled around, livid. "What do you think you're doing?" she whispered through gritted teeth as she grabbed his hand and dragged him into the living room. "How did you—?"

He shook his head and pointed next door.

"She can't hear us from in here. Talk. How did you get in here? And in the alley. And outside my windshield. Who... What are you?"

"There was an intruder in your apartment today. I followed him, but he escaped me."

Her stomach fell to her toes. "What?"

"You're involved in something perilous. You're in grave danger."

The matter-of-fact way he said those two sentences was like he was ordering a double latte with skim milk. She plopped down on the couch. "This day keeps getting better and better."

Rhune dropped to one knee and took her hands. "I vow I will not let anything happen to you."

It'd been a shit of a day, and that gallant act of kindness caused the first tear to slide down her cheek. He immediately wiped it away with the pad of his thumb.

"What's going on? I'm either going insane, or I'm caught up in some sort of nightmare and can't escape. Tell me the truth. Please. Tell me nothing but the truth."

He pursed his lips and nodded. "What I'm about to share is strictly forbidden, but you've endured enough pain and confusion. Perhaps we can figure out a solution."

She reared back. "What do mean *forbidden*?"

He took a peek at the digital clock on the coffee table. If she didn't know better, he was counting the hours. "I'm... It's difficult to explain. I have a rather unique night job."

Hanna's heart started tap-dancing. Whatever it was he was about to tell her, it was doing a number on him. She held her breath, waiting for him to continue.

"I work for God."

That did it. She jumped to her feet. "You belong to a cult! Shit and damn. I knew you were too good to be true."

"Cult?" He leaned back with his brow folded. "I don't understand. Let me explain—"

"You drugged me. Everything that's happened has been hallucinations. You've done something to me to make me join whatever group you're with." Fear riveted her feet to the carpet.

The harsh planes and angles on his face softened, and his body went limp. "I would never do such a thing to you. But you most definitely have done something to me."

Stunned, she stumbled back. She hadn't heard that right. Why would a guy like him be interested in a nothing like her?

"You are a unique individual, Hanna Carmichael, but what I need you to do right now is listen. And believe as best as you can."

She lowered herself cautiously into the cushions of the sofa. No one else knew about Roger except Rhune, and he was the only one who believed that what had happened in that alley had been real. No matter how farfetched the last couple of days had been, she needed his help. Plus, he was more than willing to give it to her. *But just how unstable is he?* she wondered.

"I'm forbidden to tell you about me because of what I am."

"What will happen if you do?"

He hesitated. "I'm not sure. I've never told anyone before."

"What are you?"

Grimacing, he ran a hand through his hair and avoided eye contact. "I'm a fable of sorts. Mortals either believe or they don't. There's never a middle ground—"

She groaned, placed her head in her hands, and mumbled, "Mortals? Oh, damn. I don't like the sound of this at all."

"You told me you've suffered from nightmares your entire life, correct?"

She lifted her head and nodded. His stare encompassed everything she wanted to keep secret. Truth be told, he was freaking her out big time, but she sensed a kinship to him she didn't understand. Why else would she have trusted this far?

"I was there."

Her heartbeat kicked up fast and loud. She barely heard herself ask, "W-What do you mean you were there? Where?"

"In your nightmares. Your eyes? Even when you were a child, they mesmerized me."

What he was insinuating couldn't be possible. She didn't want to believe him, but the earnestness carved on his face made every word credible. *How could he know?*

"I walk between two worlds, similar to you. During the day, I'm human. At night, I become something else. Something dangerous. Something only a few believe in."

He took a deep breath and let it out slowly. "I'm a hellhound. I deliver souls to Hell."

"You do what?" she asked in a croaked whisper. *How long has it been since he's had his lithium levels checked?* she wondered. A part of her wanted to laugh hysterically. The other part wanted to run like hell. Literally. And then there was this ache in her heart that kept her fixed on the couch.

"After I died, there was only one place I was going. I made a deal. Actually, I was given a gift and such gifts like that are rarely given, but the alternative? It's penance for my past sins."

She closed her eyes. *This isn't happening. And here I thought I was losing my mind. He takes the cake, and icing too.* She inched away from him, trying her best to do it as casually as possible. "You expect me to believe—"

"Last night you wore flannel pajamas with blue hearts on them. You dreamt you were on all fours in the middle of a street made up of flagstones. There was fog all around you, and the air was filled with the stench of brimstone…lots of brimstone. Something came up behind you."

She jerked upright.

"A hellhound, right?"

"H-How do you know that?"

He moved a tad closer, which made her push back into the couch.

"Because it was me. I was there. With you."

Chapter Thirteen

Hanna had a sense that every word coming out of his mouth was true, or at least Rhune believed it was, but the rational side of her couldn't fathom what he was talking about. *Hellhounds? God? Heaven and Hell?*

She'd never been religious, and the scant beliefs she did have were her own simple conceived notions of life and death. But this? Then how could she explain Rhune showing up in that alleyway? Or in front of her windshield like a ghost as she was driving seventy miles an hour? Better yet, standing inside her apartment when she'd dead-bolted the door from the inside?

The chasm that had threatened to take her down the day before opened again, only wider this time.

Her vision wavered.

Sweat beaded on her forehead.

Her heart raced.

Then Rhune did it again. He took her hands and sent that voodoo calming spell of his to ease the maelstrom of insanity brewing inside her. "You...?"

She attempted to pull free from his grasp, but he refused to let go. Perhaps it was just as well. She sensed herself falling into that deep, dark hole from which she feared she'd never return.

He gave her a small smile and continued. "After midnight, I transform into a beast that serves God, contrary to popular belief. Hellhounds ensure that the souls going to Hell are delivered. I made this sacrament to right the wrongs I'd committed in my past life. Last night, Roger was my t'elan. My target. My victim. Unfortunately, he'd made you his. Why? I don't know. Suffice it to say that his soul is where it's supposed to be."

"You a-ate him." Just saying it formed a lump the size of a brick in her throat.

"I devoured him, along with his soul, and delivered him to where he belonged. That's what we do."

"We? You mean there's more than one of you?"

"Yes, but I don't know how many. We're not a friendly family. We do what we've been entrusted to do. Nothing more. Nothing less. If paths cross, it's a nod, a cordial hello. That's it."

"What's the process? I mean, how's it all done? Do you get a secret message from God?" *Now who sounds insane?*

"It's difficult to explain. An image of the t'elan comes to me, but more importantly, their scent. I can find them without fail."

"Anywhere in the world?"

"Yes. I'm just...there. This world and the other are different. Time is nonexistent in Gehenna."

"Where's that?"

"Where you saw me last night in your dream. It's the City of the Dead."

She swallowed hard. That she could believe. "So in the alley, you received an image of Roger and *poof*, you were there?"

"It's a little more complicated than that, but yes. I've never separated myself from the beast, however. I didn't know it was even possible, but I think I sensed the danger you were in and I somehow managed to disconnect my human self from that of the hellhound."

Just as she opened her mouth, he held up his hand and stopped her. "Please don't ask how, because I haven't got an answer. I'm as perplexed about it as you are."

She sensed there were questions he wasn't going to answer, even if he had the answers. "These t'elans. They're picked by...God?"

He looked away. "Sort of. That's also a complicated process."

What isn't he telling me? "How does the process go?"

"After I transform, my job is to hunt the t'elan down. I never know who they are, what they've done, or where I go. After my first time...?"

He stopped. His face paled. "I'd begged for my memory to be wiped each morning. What I was before was gruesome, but I was neat about my kills. As a hellhound? It's utter inner chaos. The person you once were, the one granted redemption, is in a continuous battle with the hound. You don't want to do what you have to do, and that part of you knows it's your undertaking, but the hellhound side takes over. It knows nothing but death. Destruction. Its diktat. It will never stop until its t'elan is delivered. When I wake, there's nothing but flashes. Nothing substantial. And then there was you."

He paused with a shake of his head. "I felt you watching everything I did. As a child, your eyes were beacons in a dark, cold place, darker than any grave I've ever inhabited. Rainbows of the night, I used to call them. The things that I did and knowing that you witnessed them all? I tried my best to hide what I could, but it's the inherent nature of the beast. I sensed the horror you felt, but couldn't stop."

She knew exactly what he meant. Witnessing it a hundred times and more left an indelible mark. It was no wonder she wasn't more of a nutcase, although her mother had thought otherwise. However, being the one doing the acts themselves and not being able to prevent it? *No wonder he asked for his memories to be erased. But what exactly was he before his hellhound life? Something worse?* "Are you aware in that state?"

"No, not really. It's difficult to explain. I know what I'm doing, but—"

"You have no control," she said, trying to suppress a shudder.

"Yes, exactly. When I return to human form, there're only flashes of recall. Back then when I'd wake, I'd see your eyes. I always remembered them. They never vanished from my memory. Then you disappeared. I'd almost forgotten about you until..."

An awkward silence filled the small space between them.

"Until?" she pressed.

"Yesterday morning, when you woke briefly on my couch. I saw them."

He must think I'm an imbecile. "You expect me to believe that?"

For the first time, anger crossed his face. "You possess free will, Hanna. I don't. I relinquished that part of my soul when I agreed to become a hellhound. You can believe whatever you want, but I'm trying my best to explain what I can. So tell me how I would know what you were wearing last night? Or what you had dreamed about unless I was there?"

She narrowed her eyes. "You saw what I was wearing this morning."

"Then how did I know about you being in Gehenna?"

Damn it. He had a point. How could he have possibly known that? "You were in that alley and, and that thing at the same time. How?"

"As I said, I don't know. It's never happened before."

"It was going to attack you and then kill us both."

"That's its nature. It doesn't stop hunting until it completes its task. It'll take any witnesses, as well. You're alive because you weren't its target."

She felt sick. "I'm alive because of you.

"I believe so too. My being there stopped whatever was supposed to happen. Roger was my t'elan, however, someone else was controlling the hound."

"Was that how you were able to separate yourself?"

"Perhaps." He fell silent.

She looked at the clock. Nine forty-five glowed back. He followed her gaze.

"We have a little time before I have to leave. I know you have questions, and I shall endeavor to answer what I can."

"How old are you?" The words popped out of her mouth before she had a chance to stop them. Berating herself for coming up with the most inane question of all time, she watched his brow furl.

"Centuries."

Her mouth fell open. She managed to regain some composure and asked, "You remember your past life?"

He stood and walked a few feet away. The wretchedness on his face clutched at her heart. "Yes. Those memories are part and parcel of my penance."

"In the restaurant you said you were a prince?"

"Rhune was a name I took after I crossed the veils. It seemed appropriate after the many lives I'd ruined."

"What was your first name?"

He gave a weak smile. "When I was human, I was known as Prince Vlad Tepes."

She sucked in a breath before sinking deeper into the cushions, wishing she could fall into the floor and never return.

Chapter Fourteen

He'd said enough. The shock his words had obviously caused made her all the more frightened; the one thing he didn't want to do, but he was determined to do everything possible to keep her safe, whether she wanted him to or not. "This case you're working on, who knows about it?"

"The entire city. Maybe all of North America. It's a high profile murder case. And don't change the subject. You're the first vampire? Come on. I wasn't born last week."

He refrained from smirking. "But you believe in a hellhound."

"Well, I saw that. I think."

"I wasn't the first vampire. That's a story for another time. A very long story, in fact."

Her eyes narrowed cynically. "Is that why you talk so weird?"

"I didn't know I did so. Eras tend to slip by unnoticed when you're a monster. I became a vagabond of sorts after the transition to a hellhound. When vehicles were first invented, I built the gas station. I needed a place to call home. An area that was somewhat secluded, and normal. I try to renovate the place every fifty odd years to keep up appearances."

For the first time since meeting her, Hanna smiled. A small dimple formed in her left cheek that he never noticed before.

"No offense, Rhune, but your place is a dump. A renovation is definitely in order."

"You believe me." He couldn't keep the awe from his voice.

"Do I have a choice?" she said with a sigh. "But inquiring minds need to know. Who was Dracula, really?"

He sat on the floor and rehashed through the painful memories, trying to piece them together so it would make sense. "I was happily married. Had a child. A little boy. His name was Andreis. My kingdom was vast until the Turks came and stole my son. The loss proved too great for my wife. She killed herself. Our faith believed that when someone takes their own life, their soul is destined to Purgatory. I had no hope of seeing her in any afterlife. I'd lost everything except my lands, and it became inevitable that I was about to lose those too, along with the lives of a great many of my subjects. I made a deal with a devil. In exchange, I was given the power to defeat the Turks, but at a great price."

"The thirst for blood."

He nodded. "I sustained on human blood until I grew tired of the life of darkness. One day I went out to greet the morning sunrise."

"You tried to kill yourself?"

"At the time all I wanted to do was try to join my wife. Unfortunately, the powers that be had another use for me."

"For the deaths you caused, you were going to Hell, not Purgatory, right?"

"Yes. And no one better deserved such a fate. The centuries being a vampire had blackened my soul. There was no hope for me until—"

"God spoke to you?"

"In a sense."

"But Vlad impaled hundreds of people, maybe thousands before he was, well, turned."

He scowled. "History recounts only the vile acts. What they failed to mention is that the human Prince Vlad Tepes was not a warmonger. The Turks brought war to my doorstep. All I ever wanted was peace. I was Wallachia's prince, destined to protect and defend my kingdom and every person within it. I built that wall of dead soldiers to frighten away my enemies. To send a clear message to any future adversaries. Leave Romania, or enter at your peril. Impaled bodies didn't frighten the Turks, even when the majority of them were their own men. Their armies were too great. Defeat was inevitable. I couldn't allow that to happen, so I ventured into the Carpathian Mountains in search of a warlock rumored to have great powers. I was looking for magic to defeat the impending invasion threatening my lands. What I found was a demon. A vampire. He gave me what I needed to defeat my enemies, but at a great cost to me and my people.

"In the year of our Lord 1798, I gormandized an entire village. All innocents. They were once my subjects. The very people I'd sworn to protect and serve. I'd done some vile things in my life, but that deed made my decision all the more easier. I waited for the arrival of morning. I watched the cresting sun grow bigger, brighter. It had been so long since last I'd seen it. I was stunned by its beauty; its magnificence. I accepted it was the end for me. As the sunlight hit upon my flesh, I relished in the flames, the agony—the cleansing I felt."

He closed his eyes, reliving it all again. "I saw a bright light. Words were spoken. An angel came. A deal was struck. Rhune was born."

"Wow. You could take that story to Hollywood and make a blockbuster movie."

He opened his eyes. "It's my story, and I'd rather it not be shared. You must swear to never divulge this to anyone."

"Okay, I swear. No one would believe it, anyway. By the way, what will happen if I do?"

"Perhaps it's best *we* don't know."

She gulped.

"Now who is Hanna Carmichael?"

"What do you mean?"

"I've shown you mine, you show me yours, so to speak. Tell me about yourself."

Her face blossomed with color. "There's not much to tell. Your story is far more interesting."

"I doubt that," he said with a smile.

"Well, I'm nobody, really. I've suffered from insomnia my entire life, but it was because I didn't want to go to sleep. My nightmares?" She paused with a shudder. "My mother would tell me that even as a baby, I'd wake screaming and absolutely terrified. I fought going to sleep. I didn't want to see what happened in my dreams. As I grew older, my mother thought I had mental issues. I was taken to a multitude of doctors, who analyzed me and my dreams as some horrible secret buried deep in my subconscious. Then she accused my father of molesting me. It caused such a rift between them that they separated. He died shortly after of a heart attack. Then came the drugs. Lots and lots of drugs. My mother medicated me for years. Cough medicine. Over the counter sleeping aids. Her pills. Booze. It's a wonder I'm not an addict.

"At seventeen, I graduated high school and left home. I put the drug abuse behind me. My mother passed away two and half years ago from breast cancer. With what little money she left me, I went to college. I found a great job at the district attorney's office where I'm at now, and the long hours of paralegal work keep me sane. I average about five hours of sleep a night without any medication, and those are good nights. I'm thankful for them, too. Depending on how busy I am at the office, I can stay awake for about forty-eight hours before hallucinations begin. Then I crash. Big time. That's how I usually spend my weekends. In that state, I don't dream."

She gave a nervous chuckle. "So there you have it. That's little ol' me in a nutshell. Boring and sleep deprived."

He wanted to wring her mother's neck. How could someone treat their child like that? "That's how you live?"

"That's how I survive. Big difference. That's an insomniac. Unfortunately, the nightmares I'd been running away from my entire life have now become reality."

The pain she tried so desperately to conceal tore strips off his heart. No one should have had to endure such a life. Especially someone as sweet and as innocent as her.

She leaned back, her inquisitive stare searching his face. "What you just told me? I have to say it's absolutely ludicrous, but I don't know what to believe anymore. You believe it. I know that. And, well, I believe you. After what I've seen?" She hesitated. "You've done nothing but try to help me. I understand that much. And thank you, by the way, but it doesn't change the fact that I'm pretty sure I need a CAT scan as soon as possible. You're telling me the truth, or what you believe is the truth. I can sense that. However screwed up this is, you're not going to desert me, or drug me, or have me committed."

"I would do no such thing to you." He hoped his voice didn't convey what his heart was having a difficult time hiding.

"My boss wants me to find Roger."

Rhune took another glance at the clock and did a hasty calculation. "You can't be near me when I—"

"Why?"

Dumbfounded, he discovered he didn't have an answer. He'd always made sure no one was around at night. His secret was his own. He'd carried it for so many centuries, it'd become as natural as breathing. *What would she see?* he wondered.

Suddenly, a spasm of *something* raced through his nerves, like ice water being poured through his veins. He'd felt it before, but this time it was much more distinct.

He jumped to his feet and circled the room. Fury blazed as hot as Hell itself. "Did you feel that?" he enunciated between clenched teeth.

"N-No."

When he caught her expression, another chunk tore from his heart. "Hanna, you have nothing to fear from me. On my honor and word."

"What just happened?"

He couldn't muster an answer.

"Right now. Tell me why you jumped up like that."

"I'd felt something similar in the restaurant with you yesterday. It happened again. Now." He ran a hand over his hair in frustration. "It was stronger, though."

"What was?"

"Dark magic."

Chapter Fifteen

He howled at the useless smoke rising from the urn. This happening not once, but twice confounded him to no end. Hanna's aura had always been like an open book, so easy to see and manipulate, and the reason why he'd chosen her. She was a nobody, with no friends or family. His plan was too close to completion for this to happen now.

Something, or someone, had shielded the paralegal.

Who? How?

He had to get that woman out of the equation. It was all part and parcel of the plan. And where was that maggot, Simmons? He'd left a dozen messages on the disposable cell he'd given him. None of them returned. He'd even driven out to Rio-Morden and couldn't find the sleaze-ball anywhere. Next, he'd stopped at Hanna's motel room and turned the place upside down trying to find that statement of Roger's, but he'd found nothing. Not even her briefcase.

Uneasiness slithered like a nest of snakes in his guts.

Where's Simmons?

He'd hightailed it out of that dump of a town and drove back to the city before anyone could be the wiser. When he'd passed a tow-truck on the highway, some sixth-sense made him look in his rearview mirror, but he'd been going too fast to make out its occupants.

He had found nothing but dead ends. And he despised dead ends, especially with so many loose ones hanging about.

Hanna-Goody-Two-Shoes needed to be eliminated. Plain and simple. There could be no trail back to him.

The door opened behind him.

"Any luck?"

Without turning in his chair, he snipped, "If there was, would I still be in here?"

"Sorry. Maybe she has magic too?"

He shifted slowly and eyed the woman in disdain. "Then you're about as stupid as she is."

Her face flushed, but she held her tongue, which was a first.

He took a deep breath and let it out slowly. "The guy you hired. Rod? He called earlier and said someone had followed him into Hanna's apartment this afternoon."

She grinned. "If it's a male persuasion, then let me deal with him."

Good point, you little tart. "Do what you have to do."

"My pleasure." She started to leave the office.

"Where's Rod now?" he asked, stopping her in her tracks.

"Pushing up the seaweed. Whoever saw him in Hanna's apartment won't be able to recognize him. Neither will his mother," she added with a sinister grin.

"Good. Don't fail me like Simmons. Do I make myself clear?"

"Crystal." She left without another word.

She'll be another loose end. All in good time.

Dark magic? Did he just say that? Then how did Hanna explain everything that had happened? *Well, you can't, can you?*

She'd always based her life on Occam's Razor. The simplest explanation was probably the correct one. Her nightmares had been brought on by lack of sleep.

The brain did funny things when deprived of rest. But there was nothing logical about any of this.

When Rhune looked at the clock for the umpteenth time, she had to ask, "Am I keeping you from something?"

"I have only until about midnight before..." He looked away.

Before he becomes devil-dog. She shivered at the memory of him in the alley and mustered a quiet, "Right."

"Do you have a way of gaining entrance into your office this time of night?"

Where the heck is he going with this? "Yes, I have a key, and the security code."

"Do you think there might be some information there that may help in identifying why you've become a t'elan, I mean, target?"

"Sorry to burst your bubble, Rhune, but I'm pretty sure you're not going to find anything remotely close to black magic there. It's a litigious office. Nothing but suits. And lawsuits."

When his brow furrowed, it was obvious her attempt at a joke fell short. Still, she wanted to hug the stuffing out of him. This man was actually going to help her. This gorgeous hunk of a man, who happened to turn into a demon dog and deliver souls to Hell for God, mind you. When she mapped it out in her head, she was definitely booking a CAT scan. But what better protection could she have?

He must have seen the relief on her face because he offered her an encouraging smile and said, "Let's go."

Hanna didn't know why she felt like a criminal, but she did. Going to the office this late at night to snoop around instead of work didn't sit right. The only law she'd ever broken before meeting Rhune was when she got a speeding ticket in her friend's car. In under one day, she'd lied to a Sheriff, was an accessory to a crime, and not just any crime, but the murder of Roger-the-Creep, and now here she was sneaking into the offices of the people who controlled her livelihood.

Once inside, she hurried to the alarm panel and keyed in the access code. When the light turned green, she let out a lungful of air she hadn't realized she'd been holding in. Rhune towered over her, his keen gaze searching every hallway and shadow. She swore that if someone were to stab him, the rigidness of his body would have broken the blade.

"Where's your office?" he hissed.

She frowned. "I have a cubicle. Paralegals don't warrant an office."

He said nothing as he followed her toward the back of the building. Then he took her hand. His large palm swallowed hers, hot to the touch and slightly calloused. A man's hands that could stroke her skin with tenderness...and kill viciously. Her thoughts almost got away with her until...

"Doing some late night paralegaling, are we?"

Hanna jumped with a squeak and turned.

There stood Tiffany silhouetted by the lone light coming from the reception desk. One of her hands rested on her hip as she leaned with the other against the granite front. When she caught sight of Rhune, she immediately straightened. The usual condescending sneer she always sported for Hanna turned into a smile that went from ear-to-ear. "My, my, my, Hanna. Where have you been hiding him?"

She strutted toward them with her hand held out. "Hi, I'm Tiffany."

Before Hanna could retort, Rhune stepped in front and saved the day. "Good evening, Miss Tiffany. Hanna had some work she needed to pick up. I came with her to ensure her safety this late at night."

When she saw that he refused to shake the receptionist's hand, Hanna suppressed a grin.

Tiffany's eyes had widened before, but now those baby-blues of hers almost popped out of her head. "Excuse me?"

"It's a pleasure to meet you, but we're in a hurry. Hanna's quite adamant about her work, as you know. If you'll excuse us?"

Rhune didn't wait for an answer. He took Hanna's arm and steered her away from the wench, even though he had no idea where he was going.

Hanna took his cue and headed straight for her cubicle. The heat of Tiffany's stunned stare drilled into the middle of her back. It was difficult, but she managed to stifle a round of giggles that wanted so desperately to escape. He'd insulted Tiffany in the most politest of ways, and that parting expression on the woman's face had been worth its weight in diamonds.

"You know the office's protocols. Be sure to set the security alarm when you leave," Hanna called out over her shoulder.

She would have given anything to see the woman's face right then, but she didn't dare. Seconds later, the *beep-beep* of the office alarm sounded, followed by the bang of the heavy glass doors closing.

"There's something wrong with that woman."

She grimaced. "Do you want a list? She's the biggest bitch this side of the city. And I also know what she's doing here at this time of the night. She's messing around with one of the lawyers."

He glanced around the gloomy office and hesitated when he saw the clock on the wall. "That's not what I meant," he muttered under his breath. "She's...distorted."

Maybe it was his tone and the odd word he used to describe her. Or perhaps it was the cold mantle of doom that suddenly settled on her shoulders after that sentence left his lips. "W—?"

Rhune was fast. One minute he was beside her, the next he stood in front of her, protector that he was, growling like a beast. The demonic sound made every hair on her body stand at attention.

Rhune suddenly let out a high-pitched whimper and fell to all fours.

"Down boy."

Hanna jumped a foot in the air at the sound of the voice coming from the shadows. A man stepped out into the light. She blinked, and blinked again. "M-Mr. Winford?"

Chapter Sixteen

Winford's ironclad grip on Hanna's arm left bruises as he dragged her from the elevator and into his office. Rhune followed doggie style—literally—on his hands and knees, completely subservient and silent.

After closing his office door, Winford threw her into the chair opposite his desk. Then he tied her up and gagged her before leisurely taking his seat.

Every so often a subdued grunt came from Rhune. Out of the corner of her eye, she saw him facing the wall like an insolent child.

Winford didn't say a word for the longest time. He merely stared at her while bending a paperclip between his fingers. It was beyond unnerving.

"Well, haven't you become a thorn in my side," he said at last.

Hanna tried to shift to a more comfortable position, but it was useless. The sockets of her shoulders burned from being pulled behind her, so she pushed forward a bit to take the pressure off her arms. Nothing worked. She knew she looked like a deer caught on the railroad tracks with a train coming straight at her. And that train had a name. Stanley Winford, lawyer extraordinaire. No matter how many ways she attacked the situation, she couldn't fathom how he was involved. Adam Drysdale had been his best friend.

The lawyer's head did a slow turn toward Rhune. "A hellhound in the flesh. Will wonders never cease?" He shifted back. "Then there's you. And here I thought you'd be the most expendable."

At that word, rage filled her. Sure, they used her at this office, however a girl had to eat. But *expendable* as in life? That pissed her off.

"As you know, I have a reputation to maintain. But you, Hanna? You're nothing. Merely a speck of dust. You were just in the right place at the right time. I needed a rabbit to kill a wolf, so to speak. Namely, Roger." He gave a blasé shrug.

Hanna glared at the photograph of his wife and daughter, wondering if they knew what a prick he truly was.

Winford followed her gaze. "Oh yes. The joys of being married and shackled with a child. Wanda didn't understand. Neither did Adam."

His icy smirk chilled her to the marrow as understanding hit her like an anvil. *He murdered Drysdale!*

"I see the confusion in those amazing eyes of yours, so I'll elaborate. You're not going to be telling anyone about it anyway. And such a brilliant plan, too."

He paused and gave her the coldest sneer. "Several years ago, before you graced this company with your presence, and I was in private practice, I was hired by a client. A very special client. A voodoo priestess to be exact. Her practice included the slaughtering of animals. Activists wanted her behind bars for cruelty to animals. Although based on religious beliefs, that's not what outraged the public. She was politically tied to the mayor. His half-sister, actually.

"Money buys a lot of things in this city, but a secret like that can wreak havoc on someone's reputation, and career. The mayor wanted her gone, although our exact understanding of those words could be debatable. In my interviews with Samria, I began learning a great deal about voodoo."

Voodoo? Has the entire world gone insane?

"Now an interesting fact about Samria," he continued, "is she had a big mouth. She went on and on about this spell book of hers and how powerful she was. I asked to see it. Best book I ever read. It was easy enough to hire someone to make her disappear. That's where Roger came in. Another one of my past clients;

a low-life willing to do anything for the good old American dollar. After her acquittal, Samria moved back to New Orleans, or so people were led to believe. The mayor was happy, and I was paid handsomely for my services. In fact, I even got a promotion to these here lovely offices. Gotta love happy endings. Anything can be bought for a price, Hanna. *Anything*. Shortly after that, I was working late one night here and I decided to try something outlandish. Wouldn't you know it? The damn spell worked. Voodoo magic."

He chuckled. "Unfortunately, the incantation didn't go as I'd planned. I was inexperienced back then, but it got the job done. Sort of. Poor Wanda. She'll never be the same again. And with my job, I don't have time to care for her, or a child, so that worked out wonderfully, too. An inconsequential price for my freedom, I must say."

Hanna tried to tell him exactly what she thought, but all she could achieve was muffled nonsense.

Winford leaned across the desk and yanked the duct tape from her mouth.

She wouldn't need an esthetician any time soon. Every hair on her upper lip and chin went with it. Her eyes watered. "Y-You're insane!"

"I beg to differ," he replied drily.

There was no use arguing with him, so she attempted another route. "Look, let Rhune go. He has nothing to do with this."

Winford gave a rueful shake of his head and laughed. "The peon paralegal."

The insult stung deeper than the first one had, but she'd never let him know. "I don't understand what's going on."

He tilted his head toward the corner. "Your friend there has *everything* to do with this. Who do you think called the hellhound to Roger? That little shit had been blackmailing me for years because of Samria. I knew an opportunity would come where I could get rid of him. And it did. I just had to make sure my ass stayed squeaky clean. No one could know I killed Adam. After Roger disappeared, there'd be zero evidence to Samria. To Adam. To everything. Except for one little snag. You. You were supposed to be dead by the time the hellhound arrived in the alley. Roger assured me everything would go smoothly. I haven't been able to figure out how you escaped, but you're going to tell me now."

The scene in the alley replayed through her mind like a bad horror flick. *He must have used voodoo magic to separate Rhune from his hellhound.* She ignored his question and asked, "Why did you murder Mr. Drysdale? He was your friend."

That sneer of his returned frostier than ever. "You've seen my wife. I married her because of her family's money. Try living with that dead fish. I was having an affair. Adam found out about it. Simple as that. Unfortunately, he was also the one who introduced Wanda to me, *and* he prepared the pre-nuptial agreement."

He paused and gave another fleeting glance at Rhune. "I'd been drinking that night. One thing led to another. My reputation was on the line. Plus, there was the prenup to think about. If I strayed in my marital duties, I got nothing. My fingerprints were at the scene, of course, but I'd been invited there so many times before, the police never suspected me. Not his best friend who would turn the world on its head to find his killer and bring him to justice. The fire did the rest."

"But your daughter—"

"She's in boarding school in Europe. Wanda hired nannies to do the work a mother should have."

"But you're her father!" Aghast, Hanna wished her hands were free so she could punch the living daylights out of him. She had a pretty shitty childhood, but that poor girl in the photograph didn't deserve this. Never in a million years would she have guessed this man could be so cold. So uncaring. So evil. *He is a damn robot.*

"I'm her father in name only. Wanda refused a paternity test. I'd fucked her once on our wedding night." He gave a shudder.

Suddenly, his eyes widened and continued to do so until they rolled into the back of his head. The veins on his forehead and along his neck began to bulge. His body went rigid. His hands trembled as they reached up and clenched the edges of his desk. His knuckles whitened. Sweat dotted his forehead and began to run down his face in rivulets.

Through it all, he didn't utter a word. His face turned red. Then purple. And finally, blue.

Hanna watched it happen in slow motion. She tried to push her chair back, but it barely moved over the thick carpet. When Winford's eyes glazed over, she knew he was dead.

Unable to understand what just happened, she struggled with the tie holding her hands together, but only made the plastic dig deeper into her flesh. She'd be stuck there until the morning when people came into the office. She looked at Rhune, but he was still caught in that weird spell. But how? The man who'd put him in it was dead, wasn't he?

A few seconds later the door to the office opened. Tiffany's streaked black-blonde hair and baby-blues peeked over a large bag of Chinese food she carried in her arms. Using one of her high heels to close the door behind her, she nailed Hanna with a charming smile before shifting slowly in Rhune's direction.

Jealousy sizzled inside Hanna.

The receptionist strolled to the desk. She placed the take-out bag down and stared right at Winford. Then she cocked her head from side-to-side as if studying a piece of sculpted art.

Stunned, and disgusted, Hanna couldn't stop staring at him either. The color of his face was dreadful. His mouth hung just wide enough to see his black, swollen tongue.

And Tiffany? She didn't bat a fake eyelash. Beside the paper bag, the receptionist placed a deformed rudimentary doll made from stained burlap with a red silken string tied tightly around its neck.

"Sorry for the wait. The line at *Hu's on First* was positively dreadful." Tiffany paused and gave Rhune another long look.

He remained as docile as ever, still on his hands and knees facing the corner.

She grinned. "That won't do, although the view from this angle is fantastic. Don't you agree, Hanna?" With a twist of her wrist, Rhune bolted to his feet and was forced to turn.

He stood like a Christmas nutcracker statue, but his eyes? He glowered at Tiffany. For the first time Hanna realized those red flecks in them were actually tiny flames moving as if caught in a slight breeze.

"Much better. Now I can see that handsome face of yours," Tiffany said with a childish giggle.

Hanna was too stunned to speak. Winford was dead in the opposite chair; Tiffany acted like it was just another day at the office; and she had the power to make Rhune do whatever she wanted him to do. She was trapped in one of her nightmares. That would explain it. It *had* to explain it.

"You can close your mouth any time now, Hanna dear."

She didn't know it hung open. She snapped it shut so fast, she bit her tongue.

"You and your fat friend, Darla, have been dying to find out who I've been fucking. Well, ta-da!" She spread out her arms and pointed a red manicured nail at Winford. "He used to tell me what a dead lay his wife was. For fuck's sake! He couldn't find my clit even if I drew a map to it for him. I'm sure he told you all about

Adam and Roger. He did like to brag. The key word here being 'did.' Glad I won't have to listen to any more of his bullshit. What he probably didn't tell you, I'm sure, is that we both were at Drysdale's summer home the night he was killed. Adam came in unexpectedly and caught us in bed. One thing led to another and—*bang*. He was dead. I didn't shoot him, but I was an accessory after the fact—"

Hanna couldn't keep the sarcasm in. "That's a pretty big legal term for a receptionist. You sure you know what it means?"

Tiffany's face darkened. "Do I have to remind you who's tied up here? Think before you speak, bitch. Now, where was I? Oh yes. Fortunately for me, Stanley thought he'd begin to treat me like a piece of shit. Everything was going so smoothly until that night."

She stopped with a theatrical sigh and fingered the doll on the desk. "He was dabbling in powers he had no idea how to use or control. My mama practiced voodoo, and I'd learned a thing or two during my lifetime. One of them was fucking. The other, a few magical spells. And that special book of Samria's turned out to be the cat's meow. All's well that ends well."

Tiffany propped her ass on the edge of Winford's desk and examined a cuticle before continuing. "What Stanley didn't know was Samria was a fount of information to me as well, especially after I gave her the sob story of my upbringing. Stan thought he controlled the hound. Hell, he could barely control his bladder. I bided my time. After he killed Drysdale, I blackmailed him into depositing a hundred gees in my bank account to keep my mouth shut. You see, I knew I was next on his shit list. But you had to go first. And here you are. All fresh and alive-like, and with the most gorgeous man I've ever laid eyes on."

She turned and focused on Rhune. "Who are you?" she asked sweetly.

"He's... He's my boyfriend," Hanna blurted out.

Tiffany gave a heartless laugh. "You're a horrible liar, Hanna. There's no way he's your boyfriend. Look at you, for Christ's sake."

She'd had enough of the insults, but before she could retort, Rhune grunted something that caught the receptionist's attention.

The woman flicked her wrist in his direction again.

"You will release me. Now."

Rhune's husky voice made ice water trickle down Hanna's spine.

Tiffany eyes rounded, then she burst out laughing. "Well, lather me up and fuck me 'til Tuesday. You're the hellhound? This is too good to be true. Now I know for sure he isn't your boyfriend. This is going to be so much fun."

"Come to me," he whispered in the most seductive voice Hanna had ever heard come from a man. Her panties instantly dampened. And she wasn't the only one.

"Come to me," he repeated, never once looking away from Tiffany.

Whatever qualms Hanna had before about all this incantation crap, she one hundred percent believed it now. Magic swirled in the air as pinpricks of light—thousands of them. She actually witnessed the spell Rhune worked on the receptionist.

Tiffany stiffened and moved as if sleepwalking. Woodenly, she approached Rhune. Before Hanna could open her mouth, he glanced her way. The grief in his eyes struck her speechless.

"Go to sleep," he whispered.

Hanna's eyelids began to close, and there wasn't a damn thing she could do to stop them.

Chapter Seventeen

To Hanna's dismay, she found herself transported back to that hellish world of orange mist and the strange flagstone street—the place Rhune called the City of the Dead. Tendrils of fog reached for her, its touch cold and death-like. The concentrated stench of brimstone singed her nose. She discovered herself on all fours, just as Rhune had been positioned in Winford's office. *Holy crap! Is everyone supposed to be a dog in Hell?*

She blinked.

Hanna then found herself in the middle of a field devoid of any real color. The bleak scenery stretched for miles. Charred tree roots grew upward as if the trees' branches were hidden underground. The oddities were the only life in an otherwise desolate landscape. Clouds the color of slag dotted a slightly reddish-black sky that gave off no light whatsoever. *What the...?*

Her thoughts shattered as a round of demonic howls rent through the stillness. Shivering uncontrollably, she snuck a peek over her shoulder. In the distance, three large beasts sprinted in a line straight for her.

Terror rooted her to the spot. Those strange upside-down trees didn't offer one iota of protection or concealment. This was it. She was going to die. In Hell. Alone. Tears leaked from the corners of her eyes as she squeezed them shut. After several long seconds passed and nothing happened, she opened them.

The hellhounds sat in a semi-circle, regarding her with more than mere interest. This close she noticed their coat-like armor was the color of varying degrees of ash. Their eyes, large and fire filled, studied her with keen interest, but it didn't alleviate her fear. She began to hyperventilate. *If I pass out, then I won't know what happens to me.* The thought brought little comfort.

The demon-dogs did nothing but continue to stare. After several long, torrid minutes, she'd had enough. "What do you want? If you're going to eat me, then do it. Get it over with already!"

She wasn't expecting an answer, so when one came, she fell promptly on her ass in shock.

"Cerberus requests an audience with you."

"W—?"

All three beasts turned fluidly as one and began heading in the direction they'd come from.

As she struggled to her feet, she thought about running the other way, but as soon as the notion entered her head, one of the hounds stopped and turned. The menacing growl he emitted made her bury the foolhardy idea. *No use pissing them off. Who's this Cerberus? And where's Rhune and Tiffany?*

As she strained to put one foot in front of the other, the ground began rushing by. If she didn't know better, she'd swear there was a moving sidewalk beneath the ochre dirt that swirled about and coated her shoes.

She blinked.

Now she was on the same deserted street as before, but the fog was thicker and much colder. Dark shapes slinked within the shadows, but never fully formed. Before fear took over...

She blinked again.

Hanna stood in the center of four pillars of fire that burned upward and disappeared into blackish smoke. There was no ceiling or sky. Just infinite darkness. Each pillar evenly circumvented a round chamber made from the darkest granite she'd ever seen. She looked at her feet and swayed. Instant vertigo made her stomach tumble. *Why's the floor moving?*

It took a moment to realize that beneath her were thousands and thousands of mutilated, charred bodies moving listlessly in an obscene, sensuous waltz. Patches of their flesh glowed like burning embers, and their skull-like faces revealed horror she was all too familiar with. Their open mouths screamed things she couldn't hear while their skeletal arms reached up as if trying to pull her down with them.

She attempted to step back, but they were everywhere. They coiled and meshed beneath her feet. Hoping she wouldn't puke, she forced herself to look away.

Through the aberrant mist a platform materialized, rising from the floor some fifty feet ahead of her. Two of the demon dogs that had escorted her sat one at each corner. The other positioned itself beside a tasseled pillow of blood-red set in its center.

When a massive hellhound with three heads came forward through the haze and arranged itself comfortably on the cushion with all the dignity and reverence of a king sitting upon a throne, Hanna almost peed herself.

Without a doubt, this had to be Cerberus.

She blinked.

Tiffany suddenly appeared bound with thick rope that connected her hands behind her back to her ankles. As the woman stood at that awkward angle, Hanna cringed, knowing how painful it was. She'd been similarly bound not that long ago. *How much time has passed since Winford's death?* she wondered.

The hellhound with three heads leveled his fiery gazes on Tiffany. "I am Cerberus, First Captain of Gehenna. You tamper with worlds you have no right to touch."

To her shock, Hanna understood the guttural language being spoken.

"RELEASE ME!"

Hanna recoiled. Tiffany had an annoying voice, but what came out of that woman's mouth now wasn't the same she was used to hearing.

"You dare make demands when no quarter has been given?" Cerberus growled.

She realized that this hellhound's three heads spoke as if they were one and the same. The beast's voice rumbled through Hanna's body to chip away at any resolve she had left. *Stop pissing him off, you idiot*, she inwardly scolded Tiffany.

Then the receptionist's head jerked back and she screamed so loud, tears welled in Hanna's eyes.

Cerberus wasn't like Rhune. Never in a million years could she see him being this cruel. Suddenly, Roger's death came to mind. *But Rhune was in the alley with me. That hellhound who ate him hadn't been him. It couldn't have been. And if it was, Winford had been controlling him. Or had it been Tiffany? Then how do you explain all those years of nightmares watching him rip apart people?* She felt instantly ill.

What felt like hours later, Tiffany slumped to the ground, quiet at last, except for the occasional muted whimper and sniffle.

Hanna took a timid step forward. "Please stop."

Cerberus' heads lifted with distinct rumbles and snarls. It was as if they saw her for the first time. "You. Step closer."

She didn't want to, but she forced one foot in front of the other. Her body shook with dread. She had a sense that if she disobeyed she'd be beside Tiffany on the floor similarly bound. "Please. She may be a bitch, but she doesn't deserve to be tortured."

The two demon dogs sitting on either side of the platform tilted their heads and glanced questionably at Cerberus before turning their attention back to her.

The three-headed hellhound scrutinized her for the longest time and chuckled, the sound likened to metal grinding on metal. "You would spare her life knowing she intended to dispense with yours?"

Okay, she knew the woman was evil and capable of murder. Winford was evidence to that fact too, but she didn't believe in torture. Everyone deserved a second chance. She lifted her chin in false bravado. "Punish her, yes. Not torture. We all make mistakes."

Cerberus' heads reared back, each laughing hysterically. Her skin crawled as the sound thundered throughout the chamber.

"Those mistakes," he said at last, "are what bring you here. Your hands are presently clean,

Deathwalker, but you shouldn't be here. However, because of the harms this one has perpetrated upon you, I will allow you to stand witness. Know this. Her sins cannot be undone."

Deathwalker?

One of Cerberus' heads tilted as if sensing her confusion.

"Don't we all have the opportunity to right the wrongs we've done and be forgiven? Isn't that what the bible preaches?" Hanna asked hesitantly.

"There's no redemption for the taking of another life. It's why she's here."

"But Stan Winford killed several people. What Tiffany did to him, doesn't that kinda right that wrong?" She knew she was insane for trying to barter for Tiffany's life, but she didn't want to see her devoured like Roger had been. If she had to witness something like that again, she'd go insane—and she was pretty close to being there already.

"Look down."

"No," she whispered. That was the last thing she wanted to do.

"I said look down," Cerberus demanded.

She peered at her feet and swallowed hard. The bodies below were now moving in a frenzied state.

"You stand at the gates of Tartarus. Here is the entrance to Purgatory, and beyond, Hell. Few mortals have stood where you are and have continued to live."

"Is that why you called me a Deathwalker?"

A moment of uncertainty dimmed the fire in all its eyes. "You are more than a walker of the veils, woman.

You see more than any human. You are mortal, yes, but in this world, you have not changed in the centuries I've been bound here. You are ageless."

"What? I'm only thirty-two for goodness sake. That's not possible."

The hellhound sneered. "Your soul is eons old, Deathwalker. Even older than I."

Chapter Eighteen

She was definitely going to get her hearing checked when she went for her CAT scan because she hadn't heard him right.

"It's not for you to decide this woman's fate," Cerberus continued. "Judgment has been rendered. Deliver the t'elan."

Tiffany, who'd been silent up until then, began to bawl. "No! I'm sorry. Listen to Hanna. I'll be good. I promise. I repent. I repent. Please. I'll go to church every Sunday. I'll pray all day. Don't do this! Please."

One of the smaller hellhounds bounded off the step and grabbed her by the scruff of the neck like a mother cat hauling away her kitten. He shook Tiffany like a rag doll. Droplets of blood splattered across Hanna's face. Then the floor beneath his paws opened, yet he didn't fall in.

Frozen in fear, Hanna looked on in horror. The blood dripping from Tiffany's neck stained the collar of her blouse crimson. Still she fought, thrashing and twisting in the hellhound's pit-bull hold. He then pitched her down into the mass of shifting cadavers. All she could see was Tiffany's hand desperately reaching upward.

Without thinking, Hanna raced to her and dropped to her knees. She grabbed Tiffany's arm, and with all her strength, she pulled the woman up.

Demonic howls rang out.

She had no idea why she did what she did. Sure, Tiffany had made her life miserable. Sure, the bitch planned on killing her. Whatever the case, Hanna didn't want to watch someone else die, no matter how evil they were. Two up close and personal was enough in a lifetime, not to mention all the others she'd witnessed in her nightmares while growing up. At least back then she hadn't known they'd been real.

An eerie silence had settled in the chamber. She summoned a bit of courage and looked up. The three hellhounds that had escorted her here now surrounded her. Drool leaked from their maws and hit the floor, their saliva sizzling like acid on metal. She now had a detailed view of their deadly teeth. How Tiffany was still alive was a miracle.

Cerberus walked in between the hounds with flames burning deep in the sockets of those six eyes— eyes that were wide and filled with the same shock as the other three beasts.

"Once entered, no one leaves Tartarus."

She stood slowly, hopeful that she'd get a grip on whatever small amount of courage she had left. Tiffany continued to sob on the ground by Hanna's feet. The woman's neck and lower jaw were now mutilated by the teeth and acid drool of the hellhound that had held her. Her beauty was completely marred for life. For Hanna, that was punishment enough for the woman's crimes.

She turned and stared each hellhound down before speaking. "In just a couple of days, I've seen two people die horrifically. I don't want to see a third, no matter what kind of bitch she is. Sure, Tiffany has issues. Absolutely. We all do, although some not so evil-slanted, mind you. She'll stand trial for murdering Mr. Winford. I don't know how I'll explain it, but I will. She'll confess." From the corner of her eye, she saw Tiffany vigorously nodding.

One of Cerberus' massive paws clenched and unclenched.

Hanna gulped and rushed on. "There are other forms of punishment. People say all the time that Hell's on Earth, right? Return her there and let justice take its course. She'll go to prison." *What am I talking about? I know nothing about this world. Or mine, apparently.*

The other three hounds suddenly gave Cerberus a wide berth. Really wide.

Hanna knew she'd overstepped her bounds, but she moved instinctively in front of Tiffany nonetheless, her heart pounding so fast it might very well jump out of her chest. Cerberus approached as if taking a leisurely stroll. The anger in all three pairs of eyes riveted her to the floor.

Before the scream left her mouth, one of Cerberus' heads reached behind Hanna and grabbed Tiffany in his teeth. He then tossed her to the ground.

It happened so fast, Hanna couldn't stop it. She watched the woman become swallowed by the thousands grappling to claim her. The last thing she saw was the woman's terror-filled, baby-blue eyes disappear amidst the fraying bodies eager to devour her soul.

"Leniency is not given by mere mortal pleadings. You may have the ability to walk between the veils, but you do not dictate which souls are foul and which are virtuous. Be careful, Deathwalker. Others have been put down for lesser reasons."

She blinked.

She found Rhune standing where she'd last seen him. She gawked at the floor, expecting to see those horrid bodies, but what she saw was the plush carpet of Winford's office.

"Hanna?"

Pent up rage, disgust and fear spewed forth. She ran to him and began beating on his chest with her fists. "They threw her in. How could you? How could you?" she screamed.

He grappled with her arms and somehow managed to pin her wrists down. "Hanna, listen to me. I wasn't there. On my honor and soul. I wasn't there. I was delivering a t'elan. Him." He pointed to Winford. "Not Tiffany. She was still very much alive. I was merely trying to get her away from you. I had no direction. Someone, something intervened."

"But you took her!"

"Yes, but it wasn't to Tartarus. I needed to get her out of this office. Someone negated my powers. I had no control to stop it. Then the scent of my t'elan drew me away. The beast took over."

Realization sunk in. It didn't matter who took her. Tiffany was dead, and Hanna had to live with it. That now made three deaths hanging over her head.

"That woman's path was already chosen," Rhune said softly. "I told you there was something wrong with her. Once a t'elan, there's no turning back."

"She begged, Rhune. Tiffany begged and pleaded for her life. Whatever happened to forgiveness? If you work for God, isn't that supposed to be part of his grand plan? To forgive us for our sins? What kind of God is he? "

Sadness clouded his eyes. "A benevolent God. Except to those who perpetrate evil."

Chapter Nineteen

Later that morning Mr. Wright, another district attorney, arrived at the office. Rhune took the lawyer up to Winford's office, who immediately called the police and paramedics. They followed in droves. A half-written confession sat on the desk in front of Winford, who was found hanging from the ceiling. That note hadn't been there five minutes before.

God works in mysterious ways, Rhune mused.

The letter hadn't implicated Tiffany in any way, and no one seemed to notice she was missing. In the note, Winford acknowledged he'd accidentally shot

Drysdale during a drunken argument while they were playing poker. Not wanting to ruin his career by telling the authorities the truth about what happened that night, his remorse eventually got the best of him. He also confessed to not only Adam's murder, but Samria's and Roger's as well. With the trial so close at hand, everyone assumed the guilt had become too much for him to bear.

Rhune watched as the authorities pulled a gun out from one of Winford's desk drawers. Forensics would later confirm it had been the weapon that killed Drysdale. Everything neatly explained.

Except for Tiffany.

He knew that when the office reopened after Winford's funeral, and she was still nowhere to be found, people would talk. They always did. Some would speculate she and Winford had been having an affair. So distraught over his suicide, Tiffany left the city of Cordelle. Perhaps even the country.

No one would ever know what truly happened—except him and Hanna.

When the police asked to question Hanna, Rhune knew she was in no shape to give a statement, so he explained what he could to them. Thankfully, they kept their questions short. He told the detective he'd taken Hanna to work early for her to prepare for the upcoming Drysdale trial, and that she was the one who'd found Winford hanging in his office. Her distress on finding him was so believable that the police sent them home and asked that she come back to the station to make a formal statement when she was better able to do so.

One of the detectives was a little suspicious of him, but he told the police officer he was her boyfriend, that she'd forgotten her lunch, and he'd come back to the office to drop it off for her. That's when he found Hanna in hysterics.

Just like in the Sheriff's office, the fabrication of the truth had been enough that Hanna wasn't suspected in the least.

Her alibi was golden.

In the taxi ride home, Rhune held her shuddering body against his chest, hoping to calm and give her comfort. Nothing worked. Then he kissed her gently on the lips and whispered, "Rest, Hanna. I'm here. Nothing bad will happen to you ever again. I promise."

To his relief, her eyes closed, and her trembling subsided.

Then he allowed the confusion to set in.

Why wasn't I in Gehenna with her?

What had been said to her?

And by whom?

Why wasn't I summoned to take Tiffany with Winford to Tartarus?

A multitude of questions—nary an answer.

After they arrived at her apartment, he paid the driver, carried her up to her room, and tucked her into bed. Then he watched her sleep. Damn, she was beautiful, even without seeing those stunning eyes of hers. The more he stared at her, the more his heart ached.

Without realizing, he'd the lost the day. Dusky shadows filled her bedroom as the realm of night settled over their corner of the world. Still, she slept—peacefully.

He knew he'd have to leave soon, so he parked himself in the armchair across from her bed and waited. After a time, he spared a glance at the clock on her dresser. Stunned, he shifted his gaze back to her on the bed. Midnight had come and gone—and he was still here. Human. With no t'elans emblazoned on his 'to-do' list.

"What happened in Gehenna?" he whispered to the darkness. An answer came, but one he didn't expect.

"When she wakes, bring her to me."

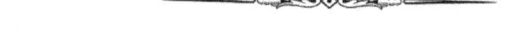

Hanna dreamed, and for the first time, there were no monsters.

No running blindly.

No nightmares.

Just blissful peace and rest.

When she woke, it took a moment for her eyes to adjust. When they did, she immediately searched the shadows and discovered Rhune sitting in the armchair in the darkest corner of her room.

Those familiar eyes with the glowing red specks brought a sense of warmth and comfort she'd come to know, and rather liked. "Hi."

He bolted forward, which caused the light from the hallway to cast a shadow across his worried face.

The fluttering of her heart made her cheeks burn. She hoped he didn't see the effect he had on her.

"How are you feeling?" he asked quietly.

"Rested. And that's very weird. I've never felt like this before."

He moved the chair closer to the edge of the bed. "You've slept for almost twenty-eight hours straight."

"I've been exhausted my entire life, Rhune. Actually, I'm kinda shocked I slept."

"I'm glad that you did."

Stilted silence followed.

"Well—" they said in unison.

"You first," Rhune cut in.

"No. You go."

Pursing his lips he settled into the chair, waiting for her to begin.

So she placed her thoughts into a somewhat coherent order and began, swallowing hard several times to maintain her nerve. "My entire life, I've never slept like a normal person, and when I did, something either chased me or it was devouring somebody. I've seen horrible, horrible things. You were there. It was always you I saw. You frightened me to the core, but what I've come to understand is it's because of *what* you are. Not *who* you are. Your job is ugly. I get it. But someone's got to do it, right? Your eyes? Like they are now? They fascinated me. Scared me shitless too, but maybe I always knew about that other world and just didn't want to believe. Who wants to be different, right? I've fought that stigma my entire life. I hate it."

She paused to nervously toy with the corner of her blanket. "I've been used, abused, ignored, and until recently, almost killed a couple times. Yet in these last couple of days since knowing you, I've never felt more alive." *Shit! I've said way too much.*

"Have you noticed the time?"

She took a quick glance at the clock. "It's one fifty-four."

"Do you remember when I told you that you're a Dreamwalker?"

She nodded. "But the other big hellhound called me a Deathwalker."

He froze. The only reaction was the fiery glints in his eyes seemed to grow more intensely. "Remember I told you that you had the ability to walk between worlds? Between the veils of life and death?"

"Yes?"

"It's a power."

"I kinda figured that out on my own. What does it mean? How does it work?"

"Some mortals possess different abilities. Walking between the veils is one of them. Most don't know they're even doing it. They believe they're dreaming or having a nightmare...like you did for all those years. Your condition? What you call insomnia? It's not. It's really a gift. You tend to feel the horror more deeply. Most Dreamwalkers don't feel emotionally connected to what they see because they make themselves believe it's not real. And even though you've tried to do the same, a part of you knew, and have always known that what was happening was actually real. At least on that side of the veils. Humans shouldn't know that."

"Is that why those hellhounds were surprised by me?"

He shrugged indifferently and looked everywhere else but at her.

What isn't he telling me? "They threw Tiffany into those thousands of dead bodies. I pulled her out, but it meant nothing. I couldn't save her."

When he looked up, the red specks in his eyes seemed to dance like fire caught in the wind. "Why did you want to save her?" he whispered.

"Because no one deserves to die like that. You didn't see her face as those *things* pulled her down. Call me a human with a heart. I don't care. She was evil. Yes. She tried to kill me. Yes. But as a human being, no matter how bad a person is, it should be inherently bred in us to try to be kind, forgiving and helpful. Tiffany wasn't like me. I get that. But if I'd stood by and did nothing, that would have made me no different than she was. Furthermore, a hellhound shouldn't be the one to administer last rites and decide where a soul goes.

"We don't, Hanna. But neither do..." He stopped.

"But neither do what?

"Nothing."

"Then Cerberus—"

"Cerberus?" He tried not to sound surprised but failed.

"He was the head hellhound. Huge. Three friggin heads! Said he was a captain. He got mad. He grabbed Tiffany and threw her into the pit anyway and…" She stopped and drew a shaky breath. "There was nothing I could do to stop it."

Something strange crossed over Rhune's face. Whatever it was, it looked somewhat painful.

"Cerberus is just and honorable. Please understand that judgment of a soul can't be decided by a mere mortal."

"That's exactly what he said! But neither should it be judged by a hellhound either." She stopped and shook her head. "You know, if someone were to eavesdrop on our conversation right now, they'd be in for a whole lot of crazy."

"Hanna—"

"You called me a Dreamwalker. Cerberus called me a Deathwalker. What's the difference?"

He said nothing, but she sensed him inwardly clashing with something.

"What am I?" she pressed.

Again, he didn't answer.

Her heartbeat kicked up a notch. "Answer me. What am I?"

"When someone dies in this world, their soul, or sometimes lack of one, becomes locked in a battle."

"I thought you go either to Heaven or Hell."

"It's not that simple."

The deadness in his voice made her stiffen. "Nothing is ever simple with you, is it?"

"I'm a hellhound. There's nothing simple in what I am, but I'll try to explain. God and Asmodeus battle for possession of that soul. In the end, it's the human that ultimately chooses."

"Are you kidding me? That's bullshit! Hell was definitely not Tiffany's choice."

"No. And please, profanity doesn't become you."

"Too bad. No, what? That you're kidding me, or no that Tiffany chose Hell?" she snapped.

"Have I ever perjured myself to you?"

There he went with those weird words again, but he had a point. He'd been nothing but truthful. And helpful. "No," she admitted begrudgingly.

"Well, I'm not about to begin now."

"So, tell me what happens after we die." *This should be good.*

"A soul will battle to stay in the world of the living. It's its nature. Only a small number of humans truly want to die. Or are ready to do so. And those people come fully prepared for the afterlife. They believe in God, or a higher power. They *know* there's a better place than Earth. Their souls are strong, which gives them the ability and strength to defeat Asmodeus."

"What do you mean defeat?"

"He's the father of deceit. He'll take a soul by whatever means possible."

"How?"

"I can't tell you."

"Well, that's damn cryptic, thank you very much, but you still haven't answered my question."

"When you pass on, then you'll understand."

"Okay, say I die. What happens to me next? Is there an interview or something? Does my life get picked through by the good deeds I've done as opposed to the bad ones?"

He shook his head, refusing to elaborate.

"Not supposed to know," she mumbled past the frustration.

"When a soul is surrendered to Hell, my job is to deliver them so they can begin their journey. Gehenna? That's a little like a train station to Purgatory's gate. Those unfortunates who took Tiffany into the ground? They're Purgatory's legions. The truly evil are always taken for a tour there first. They are the souls even Asmodeus doesn't want. Hell is Hell. Purgatory offers them a taste of what's to come."

"No! That wasn't Purgatory. It was... It was... Horrid!"

"Hell's far worse," he muttered.

All she could do was gawk back.

"You must rest."

"No. Not yet. I need answers, Rhune. Explain ghosts to me then. Why are they still here? Why haven't they been dragged to Purgatory or Hell or crossed over to Heaven?"

"Thousands die every day. Some choose to stay in eternal limbo as guardians over the ones they love. Like angels. They don't seek the light but rather veer away from it. Not all of them stay because they want to either. There's some who just get lost along the way."

"And the others?"

"Asmodeus sets them free to wreak havoc onto the mortal world. There are thousands that have crossed over into Hell. And every one of them waits at its door. They wait to be set free."

The way he said that made her shudder.

"Understand that the evil in some humans' souls can't be vanquished, not even in death. Some are just plain unrepentant. However, the penitent soul will fight for what's just. As I said, it's a mortal's soul that ultimately decides.

"But—"

He held up his hand. "I know what you're going to ask. If you stop interrupting, I'll be better able to explain. Because of the number of people that die every day, there are not enough hellhounds to deliver them all. You have to remember that our purpose is to deliver souls to either Purgatory or to Hell. Not Heaven. God has angels to do that. The souls we're entrusted with can, and do, continue their hatred long after they've passed. Hellhounds must be there at the moment of death to take the t'elan. If we're not, they can escape back into the world as poltergeists. In other words, evil reincarnate. Sometimes there just isn't enough of us."

He paused and grasped his hands together. "But you, Hanna? You shall have nothing to fear in death. Your soul is pure. I see the goodness that radiates from you as waves of incandescent light."

Blood rushed to her face. Nobody had ever said such a thing to her before. His explanation made sense, in an insane way. But it still didn't explain her power. "Really? So if I'd been successful in pulling Tiffany—?"

The sadness in his voice reached out and cradled her. "Rest, Hanna. Close your eyes and sleep."

Her vision began to blur, and her lips went numb. Unable to finish her sentence, she drifted back off to sleep.

Chapter Twenty

No sooner did Hanna's eyes close that she felt a sudden need to open them.

"You shouldn't be here."

She shifted and found Rhune in all his hellhound glory. "Yeah, you said that the last time, but here we are. The City of the Dead. Did you bring me here?" she asked. It was odd, but Rhune and this place didn't scare her like it did before. "And don't think for one moment that we're not going to finish our little talk."

"This isn't the time or place."

"No, it's not. Wait a minute. Don't you have a t'elan to deliver or something?"

Rhune started to shake his head when he suddenly reared up, peering at something over her shoulder. Hanna jumped back just as his coat of fire flared higher, and ten degrees hotter.

Too intent on trying to figure out what was going on with him, she failed to notice what was happening in the background. When she did, the first one had touched her. She recoiled, but wasn't fast enough to move in Rhune's direction. Hundreds of black tentacles reached out and wrapped around her. Their vile touch stopped every thought in her head. Cold unlike any she'd ever felt moved through her veins. Before she could scream, they latched onto her like starving leeches and pulled her backward so fast that the last thing she saw was Rhune standing about nine feet tall and howling out a sound that shook the foundation of the entire ghostly city.

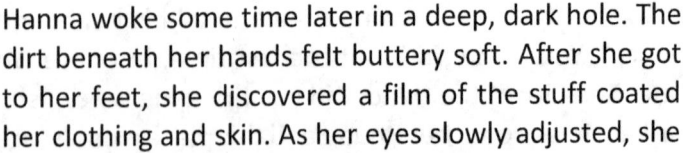

Hanna woke some time later in a deep, dark hole. The dirt beneath her hands felt buttery soft. After she got to her feet, she discovered a film of the stuff coated her clothing and skin. As her eyes slowly adjusted, she realized it was ash.

The space she was in could barely accommodate her. When she stretched out her arms, she could place her palms flat against the walls.

She looked up to see a reddish-orange glow emanating above from a small opening. Every so often, one of those creepish shadows passed overhead to block the meager light for seconds at a time. She wanted to call out for help, but fear over who or *what* might hear her jolted her common sense to remain quiet.

She had no idea where she was or who'd taken her. Those shadows in the fog had fixated on her and refused to relent.

Why?

Where was Rhune?

Was he okay?

Hanna wrapped her arms around herself and waited for whatever was going happen next. *Well here I am stuck in that dark hole I was so scared of falling into.*

Going to sleep wasn't an option. Her nerves were frayed beyond the point of being able to rest. Plus, what kind of dream would she have to endure next? A nightmare within a nightmare? She knew now that there were worse horrors than hellhounds in this Godforsaken place.

Without warning, an odd turbulence began vibrating the ground beneath her feet. The ash around her began to swirl in the stagnant air. It clogged her nose and made it difficult to breathe. Then it picked up in velocity. Faster and faster.

In seconds, a mini tornado lifted her upward toward the only exit. She grappled for balance by skimming her hands along the walls. The closer she got to freedom, the angrier she became.

She was through with people *and* monsters using and abusing her. She had powers here, and damn it, she was going to use them, whether she knew how to or not.

When she came out of the top, however, she kept right on moving. Caught in the strange vortex, she sped down long tunnels of obsidian rock and darkness. What felt like hours later, she came to an abrupt stop. Then she dropped about five feet to the ground.

She tried to breathe but the air here was putrid, like something had died and was never buried. She was getting used to these obscene smells, but right now, she'd rather have brimstone burning her nose than what was currently assaulting her senses.

Something flashed in her peripherals. Then again. She turned this way and that, but wasn't fast enough. The silence here hung on her shoulders, weighing down her limbs, and her will. Drawing in oxygen was difficult. Shadows slithered across the walls, but they were gone as quickly as they came. One thing was for certain. This wasn't Gehenna.

"Welcome, Deathwalker."

Hanna turned in a slow circle to find the source of the guttural voice.

A dry, vile chuckle followed. "Do you think your will is strong enough to look upon my face?"

She took as deep a breath as she could and let it out slowly. "I've seen some pretty disgusting things of late. Why not another?"

An aberrant glow lit up a space about ten feet away. It outlined what looked to be a tall and extremely skinny being. As the light grew brighter, the shape became clearer.

She swallowed down a scream and tried her best to be brave, but her knees wouldn't stop knocking together.

The demon that stepped closer wore no clothes. With his junk hanging out for all to see, it was definitely male. His skull was grotesque, with bits of decomposing flesh still hanging from the exposed skullcap. The body was pale, almost translucent; his arms much too long; his legs even spindlier. He looked like a holocaust victim, only ten times worse. His empty, sunken eye sockets narrowed in amusement.

Hanna looked away and swallowed a bubble of bile. The horrid smell came from him.

"Still feeling strong enough?" he mocked.

With every ounce of courage she could muster, Hanna turned back to him, raised her chin, and stared the demon down. "This is just a dream. Just another nightmare is all."

"This is more than a dream, Deathwalker. This is your reality. And future."

"No, it isn't." She swallowed again, trying to lubricate her throat. The air was so dry, it hurt to blink. "Rhune will come for me. When he does, your ass is toast."

The demon threw back his head and laughed hysterically. It was difficult to watch the tendons in his jaw stretch to the point where she thought for sure the lower half of his face would fall off. Worse was the sound of his chilling laughter. It almost made her pee her pants.

"Do you think your *pet* will save you, human?" he spat. "Where is he now?"

The same question plagued her. *Is Rhune okay?* she wondered for the hundredth time.

"That noble thinking of yours means little here. You're going to serve me, Deathwalker. Whether you want to or not."

"Like hell I am!"

She didn't know what happened next, nor did she care. She drew herself taller. Literally. She towered at least a foot over the demon and stared him down. "I will not serve you, or anyone else for that matter ever again. I'm through being a scapegoat for people, or-or whatever you are."

The demon's skeletal hand reached up and snaked around her neck. It was the alley and Roger all over again. This time Rhune wasn't there to save her.

She closed her eyes and waited to die. As the hand squeezed tighter the last thought in her mind was of Rhune and how stupid she was for not telling him how she truly felt about him.

"You *will* serve me and my many souls."

Suddenly fire was everywhere. She threw back her head and screamed as she felt her flesh began to crisp. The demon's shrill laughter filled every space of her mind. Then through the flames, she saw eyes boring into her—familiar eyes.

The demon now roared in fury. "You think you can save her? We will take her as our own, and there's nothing you can do about it, demon-dog. Mark my words.

Hanna, wake up. WAKE UP!

She found herself engulfed in flames, but this time the fire didn't hurt. Brimstone had now become her favorite scent.

"Hanna!"

The sound of Rhune's voice made her open her eyes. She didn't know a hellhound could look so wretched until this moment.

Without thinking, she wrapped herself around him. "Don't let go of me. Please. Don't ever let go of me." Then came the tears and there was no way she could stop them.

Towering flames surrounded her again, but they didn't burn. She welcomed this fire. Embraced within Rhune's warmth and safety, all she cared about was being next to him.

As he held her, she sobbed, her delicate frame shaking him to the core of his being. The multitude of questions bombarding his brain would have to wait until she was ready to talk about what had happened. He refused to push her. She'd endured too much already.

Who had taken her?

What had she endured?

And more importantly? Why?

He had an inclination. And if he were right, it would confirm his worst fears.

Can this innocent woman truly be a Deathwalker?

He wasn't allowed to speak of such things. Humans could never know the extent of such powers. To be able to take any soul and set it free into the world of the living? She'd be in danger every day of her mortal life. All kinds of demons would hunt her down to make her their own.

A plan formed. One that would be dangerous for all of them. Especially now that he had to bring her back to Gehenna to face Cerberus.

He placed Hanna gently on the bed and knelt beside her. "Shush. I'm right here. I promise I'll never leave you. Sleep, Hanna."

With a touch of his magic, he took her memory and erased hers before sending her back to the place that had done this to her. Back to the City of the Dead. But this time he was prepared. This time he'd ensure she'd be safe—forever. This time, he'd control the outcome. Especially now that he knew what she really was.

Chapter Twenty-One

Hanna woke again and found herself in the center of Gehenna's street. Same flagstones. Same eerie mist, but she wasn't alone. Even though her heart pounded against her ribcage, she had a sense she was safe.

Glints of what looked like fireflies illuminated through the fog. She had no fear as they came closer. She'd never mistake those eyes again. Rhune's eyes.

Slightly oval, but slanted upward at the corners, and filled with intelligence. Why had she not noticed them like that before? This close, she realized the glinting specks of red were actually flames.

Timidly she reached up onto her tiptoes and touched his face. His armor-like fire-fur was thick, bristly, and very warm. Not burning hot, but startling enough to draw her hand back. He moved closer and nuzzled her fingers.

She blinked.

Now she stood in the center of that barren field with the bizarre upside-down trees. She turned to ask Rhune about them, but he wasn't there anymore. Panic was about to set in until she caught sight of three familiar hellhounds loping toward her in the distance. She waited, knowing what was coming next.

"Cerberus requests an audience," they said as one voice.

Here we go again. She gave the field one last fleeting look before following them.

She blinked.

The chamber was exactly as she remembered. Cerberus sat on his throne, and the other three in their usual positions. From between the darkness of two pillars of fire on her right, Rhune came forward and stood beside her. She noticed he was bigger than the other three hounds, and only slightly smaller than

Cerberus. His coat was more the color of dark ash than Cerberus's pure black.

The large hellhound stood and came down from his platform. He circled her with each of his heads sniffing her hair and her clothes.

Rhune stared straight ahead.

"How is it that she knows of our world?" he asked Rhune.

"She was brought into our realm by means I don't understand."

"Our laws are unequivocal. We are the gatekeepers of the balance between good and evil. Only in dreams can she walk, but here she stands. Aware. Imagine my surprise when you sent her to stand witness."

Hanna took a step forward. "I begged him to tell me. It wasn't his choice."

Rhune turned to Cerberus with a growl. "I didn't send her here."

"Then who did?"

"I sent myself."

One of the heads snapped at her. "You're a poor liar, woman. Do you know who and what you are?"

She nodded. "I'm a Dreamwalker. When I sleep, I can move between the veils of the living and the dead. But you called me a Deathwalker."

"So I did. Do you know what that means?"

Confused, she shifted around to face Rhune. He looked to the ground, saying nothing. "Not really. A little, I guess. Yes."

"Therein is our conundrum." Cerberus went back to his platform and sat. "She must be destroyed."

Stunned, she stared from Rhune to Cerberus. "What?"

Rhune rose to full height. "She walks between the veils, yes, but she's tampered with nothing. There are others in the mortal world who know who and *what* they are, yet we don't destroy them."

"Yes. But they don't know they possess powers, nor have they ever used them. I've seen what she's capable of," Cerberus answered carefully. "And so has she. She cannot be set free to walk both worlds. She knows too much. She'll be given another life. In time. She's a Deathwalker. Her soul is eternal."

Hanna took a shaking step back. "I don't understand. What powers? I'm nobody. Just a paralegal. I can't even walk and blow my nose at the same time. I swear I won't say anything about what I've seen. Are you kidding? Who'd believe me anyway?"

Cerberus leveled her with three stares that laid bare her soul. "You pulled the woman from Purgatory. Only one has the power to decide such fates, and it is not you. A mere mortal. Pah!"

"You make 'mortal' sound like a disease. I tried to save her, and failed, thanks to you." She whirled round. "Rhune, what's going on?"

"It's as I told you. Souls will battle until the bitter end, even after their fate is decided." He looked positively miserable.

Hanna sensed something else was going on. Something she missed. She also sensed Rhune wasn't going to tell her, either. Or perhaps he couldn't, and that she had to figure it out on her own. So why couldn't she erase the memory of pulling Tiffany out from those vile things? Something about it was important. Worse, something else tugged at her memory. Something horrific.

She gawked from one hellhound to the other. Each of them studied her with more than a little interest. Even Rhune.

"This is another nightmare. I'm home. In bed. I'll wake up, and this won't be real."

No matter how many times she said it, she knew this was reality. Her entire life, her dreams had been filled with horrors, and she'd stood by unable to do anything but watch. *Wait. Could I have saved them?*

"A mortal has no right to determine a soul's final destination. When a decision is made, it's everlasting. No *human* can possess that kind of power. Your race is...flawed. The balance of worlds is maintained at all cost."

"Balance of worlds?" *Stop blubbering and think.*

"You, Hanna Carmichael, are an anomaly to the balance. Dreamwalkers enter behind the veils, yes, but you? You have the power to change their fates. That is a Deathwalker. When a soul is committed to Hell, you cannot alter their final destiny. You're forbidden to even try. You cannot save them. Rhune explained this, did he not?"

Standing beside him now was like being next to an inferno. She took a step sideways hoping her hair didn't catch fire. But seriously, that was the least of her worries.

"No, I didn't share that information with her. Her knowing what a Deathwalker can do is your doing. Not mine. And there's something else you should know. A demon has made a move to capture her as his own."

Stunned, she made a slow turn toward him. The tone of his voice chased shivers up and down her spine. "A what?" she whispered.

"I will not speak his name, but a few hours ago he took her," he said without looking her way. "She's strong enough to withstand even the most threatening of evils."

What's he talking about? What demon? Did Rhune plan all this?

Cerberus was on his feet immediately with all three canine features etched in disbelief. The other three hellhounds backed away.

Furious with the half-truths Rhune had given her, and now this, Hanna had had enough. If she'd known she had the power to save Tiffany, would she have done so?

She stormed toward the platform. "I could have saved her? Wasn't Purgatory enough for her? No. Apparently, you, him, whoever, condemned her to Hell. Even after she tried to repent. If God is so good and all mighty, he would have forgiven her. That's what the Bible says. That's what we *mortals* have been led to believe. I will not... No, I won't believe God could be that mean. And if he is, then to Hell with him!"

Gasps raced around the chamber.

Cerberus leaned close until all three of his muzzles were mere inches from her face. The fire in their eyes almost leaped out of their sockets. This close, the brimstone made it near impossible to draw a breath. And the heat? No doubt about it. She was going to have a sunburn.

"You seem to forget," he hissed in clouds of smoke. "He's *your* God too. Perhaps that woman's soul was darker than you knew?"

Rhune moved in between them. "She will always be in danger. The demons know who and what she is. I propose that she stay with me. I was not the one who shared the knowledge of her powers. As such, she can't be destroyed because of me. I broke no covenant. *You* must ask forbearance and direction as to what will become of her. Tell him that from this night forth, she will accompany me whenever I hunt t'elans. She shall bear witness only, and I'll ensure she never uses her powers. And never will she be far from my sight. Day or night. I oath this upon my soul."

Hanna knew her mouth hung open, but for the life of her, she couldn't remember how to close it.

Cerberus reared back, each head gawking from Rhune to her. "You're willing to do this?" he hissed.

Geeze. Staying with hunky Rhune or going back to my old life with an office full of people who'd stare and point fingers at me because I was the one who'd found Winford? Darla was her only friend in the world next to Rhune. In hindsight, it wasn't a difficult choice to make.

She lifted her head. "Yes."

Cerberus shimmered like a desert mirage and disappeared before her eyes. She took two breaths and he was back. Obviously, time worked differently here.

Each head gave a bare minimum of a nod at Rhune. "So be it."

She blinked.

They had returned to the safety of her bedroom.

She didn't have a chance to say anything. Rhune swept her into his arms and kissed her. The passion buckled her knees.

He pushed away and took a few quick steps back. "I'm sorry. I took great liberties. I apologize."

"Really?" She grabbed him fast and refused to let go.

At first his kisses were urgent, demanding, and downright powerful. Then he forced her to slow down. He tasted a little like overcooked caramel, but delicious nonetheless. He lifted her up and carried her to the bed.

"You're not going to start the sheets on fire if we do this, will you?"

"The only fire I'll start is one inside you."

She grinned. "I can live with that."

As he proceeded to kiss a path down the nape of her neck, her world stopped. All the bad that had happened in the last couple of days disappeared. Nothing mattered but him.

The warmth of his hands roaming freely over her body set passion to flame. He invoked feelings she didn't know she possessed. His deep kisses scored her very soul. She moved with him as if they'd made love their entire lives. Rhune matched her fervor with a hunger that both frightened and excited her. He devoured her in all ways possible. And she submitted in every way she knew how.

They made untamed love until the wee hours of the morning. Spent and content, she lay on his chest with a sigh. He was like a body-size hot water bottle.

This was the happiest moment of her entire miserable life.

She outlined his tattoo with her finger. "The artist did amazing scroll work. What do the keys mean?"

"One opens the gates to Gehenna. The other to Purgatory."

"Oh." She leaned up on her elbows to study his face. Something in his expression soured the moment. "What's wrong?"

He rose from the bed and slipped his jeans back on. As the flesh of his ass disappeared behind the thick denim, she emitted a contented sigh. She looked forward to seeing that every day.

Once he zipped up, he dragged the chair into the corner and sat. Hanna gathered up the blankets around her and leaned her back into the wall, waiting.

"Centuries ago, when I was human, I had been blessed to find a love I could call my own. Such a love happens but once in a lifetime. When you're as old as I am, you give up on such silly things happening again. But to find one's soul mate? You saved me, Hanna. I had loved my wife. And my people. I sacrificed myself to evil so that they may live. I sacrificed myself again to kill the evil I'd become. That's why I was offered the chance of redemption. Selflessness."

She frowned. He was spoiling the moment. "Can we talk about something else?"

"No. I must tell you this. My life after my wife's demise became dark and gruesome. I did horrendous acts. Hope? Love? Everything I cherished? Everything I held close was gone. And with it, my soul. I was destined for Hell. But because I had loved, and could love, the God you were so quick to denounce granted me salvation. But tonight...?"

He turned away. "I sacrificed more than myself. I made a rash decision without your consultation. For that, I'm deeply sorry, but it was the only thing I could do to save you. I-I didn't want to lose you."

"It's okay. I want to be with you too. I mean, if you and I are going to be living together we should be honest with each other, right?"

Her heart threatened to burst from her chest as she waited for him to continue. He loved her. A nobody like her.

"You don't know how this is to be achieved," he mumbled.

The shadows in the room seemed to darken as his face softened into sadness.

"What do I have to do?"

"You're a Deathwalker. Believe me when I say your soul is eternal. It will never die. You have the ability to choose to come back in fetal form, stay as you are now, or someone completely new.

"I don't understand."

"To fulfill the oath I made..." He stared hard at the carpet while grasping his hands tightly together. "You must pass from this world in order to enter mine."

Chapter Twenty-Two

She opened her mouth, but nothing came out.

Then she began hyperventilating. Rhune immediately moved next to her.

A thousand scenes ran through her mind. Her life. Her family. Her friends. Her job. Unfortunately, there wasn't much. In fact, it took less than a couple of seconds. Everything that was important to her was right here.

Rhune took her hand. Warmth filled her. When she looked into his eyes, she knew.

She'd always known.

"I have to share something else," he said.

She held her breath. *There's more?*

"A memory I stole from you that I must return. It's one of the reasons why I made this decision. I promised to keep you safe, and I'll hold to that vow until the end of my days." He placed the pad of his thumb against her left temple.

Her mind exploded into a myriad of lights which quickly faded to grey, then black. Within the darkness, shadowy tentacles reached for her. Demented laughter rang in her ears. Then the stench of rot filled every sense. There was such evil in the visions assaulting her mind. When her meeting with the demon came to the forefront of her thoughts, she cried until she had no more tears left to shed.

Showered and changed into clean pajamas and underwear, Hanna sat at her desk and wrote a note to her one and only friend. The guilt at leaving Darla behind without so much as goodbye didn't sit right with her. Rhune advised against it, but Hanna refused to be swayed.

Still shaking from the memory of her meeting with the demon, she put pen to hand and tried her best to explain without saying too much.

Dear Darla.

Life never happens as we expect it to. Please don't grieve for me when I'm gone. I was blessed to call you my friend, but there comes a time when one must let go. Death is merely another journey we all must take. Always fight for what's right in this world. Live life to its fullest and love large. Your soul depends on it.

I know I'm going to a better place when I die. Destiny is strange, but take comfort in knowing I'll be happy. Find true love and happiness in the small things in life, and remember me fondly.

Your friend always,

Hanna Carmichael

She wiped away her tears, folded the note and put it in her briefcase—the one place Hanna knew would be searched by the authorities.

As she lay on the bed, fear bludgeoned her from the inside out. Knowing you were about to die was daunting enough, but administering that death upon yourself was even more difficult to fathom, but she was determined that Rhune uphold his vow. And for her to continue living, she had to die first.

How screwed up was that?

This was her decision and hers alone. Deep down she knew Rhune's love would keep her safe.

She closed her eyes and listened to the sound of his voice. His husky, soft-spoken baritone weaved through her mind like silk.

"Don't force it, Hanna," he whispered. "Accept your death. Pretend you're weightless, like a feather caught in the wind."

His words lulled her deeper and deeper into a dark void. A moment of panic set in, but before it escalated, she sensed the touch of his hand in hers. That small gesture eased the rigidness of her muscles and relaxed her mind to listen more closely.

"Concentrate on your heartbeat's rhythm. Slow it down. Don't be afraid. I'm right here with you. I won't leave your side. Never. Hear my voice, Hanna, and nothing else. And don't forget me."

The deeper she went, the more intense her panic of the unknown became. It didn't help in the least that the last of his instructions echoed through the emptiness that had swallowed her.

Hanna slowed her breathing. The darkness closed in completely until there was only silence. She drifted in a vacuum of obscurity. All fear and uncertainty disappeared.

Then came the light. A radiance that saturated into every cell of her being.

Mellifluous voices whispered in the background, almost like singing. She existed of nothingness.

She felt no sadness.

No loss.

No pain.

No anger.

She'd become the luminosity and the actuality of what was uniquely her soul.

Acceptance came. She was a wisp of existence moving through time itself. An infinite mass that could circumvent both life and death.

The aversion of human memories continued to cling to her, even though she sought to set them free. Souls had no purpose of the memories of old lives.

Strange though it was, a part of her clung to one particular human; a woman named Hanna Carmichael.

A sense of being pulled backward took hold. Curious as to where it led, she soared along with the currents of winds that rushed through her metaphysical body. Flickers of oddly colored lights curtailed into the brilliance of her world.

Then everything came to a jarring stop. She looked down.

A human woman lay on a metal gurney. A male leaned over the naked female body. He hummed softly under his breath as he washed the blood from the pale flesh that had been ravaged and sewn back together. As his hands moved over the mortal's skin, his humming didn't stop. Tied around the toe of the body was the name, *Hanna Carmichael*.

The scene abruptly changed to three males lowering a long box into the ground. A few people stood around the hole in the ground, but the robust female standing to the side caught her attention. There was something familiar about her. Every so often the woman wiped away moisture that leaked down one cheek and then the other. In her hands she clenched a crumpled note.

In death, there is everlasting life. Why do mortals not understand this? the entity wondered.

Suddenly, something vile caught her awareness. It raped through the peaceful moment like a jagged piece of glass carving through her existence. Such odiousness could only be one thing.

So the underworld thinks to claim this mortal as their own. Why? What's so special about this Hanna Carmichael?

She blinked.

Raindrops had begun to fall on the freshly mounded dirt. There were no mortals around now. Night had descended on this plane called Earth. There were no signs of life. Just a stillness the entity knew all too well. In the distance, a man came running. The earnestness on his features intrigued her.

He stopped at the grave and began frantically digging. He cried out as his hands moved faster and deeper into the ground. Whispers reached for her. She wanted to be gone from this place. Such sadness was wasted on her soul, but this desperate act kindled something inside and kept her stationary. An unknown force she'd never felt before.

"Don't forget me, Hanna. Come back," the man kept repeating.

It was then she realized this was no ordinary mortal. Towering flames erupted from his body as he morphed into his true self—the form given to him by the Creator himself. Soon the fire obscured him from her sight.

Confused, she drew back as far as the odd force holding her there would allow.

Anger, frustration, loss...emotions she had no need for wrapped around her and took hold. She tried to leave, but the hellhound's need was relentless.

"Come back to me, Hanna!"

His love for this perished woman *was* the power keeping her immobile. His pain and loss scored through her.

This wasn't right. Never before had this happened.

Inquisitiveness drew her nearer. Then came the darkness. That familiar shade of oblivion she'd existed in for thousands of years.

She blinked.

Hanna opened her eyes to complete blackness. For a moment, she thought she'd gone blind. She heard scratching above her. Then a voice calling out her name. She tried to move, but the box she was in had cramped all her muscles. She called out, but her voice was nothing but a muffled cry.

Panic set in. Claustrophobia came next. She began hyperventilating, which was extracting the limited amount of oxygen too fast. She began to cry, which was the worst thing to do because the tears leaked into her ears.

The scratching above grew louder. Closer.

"Don't forget me, Hanna!"

All fear and anxiety disappeared. She recognized the voice and smiled.

Chapter Twenty-Three

Hanna walked through a field of towering

golden wheat, sighing in contentment as she ran her hands along the tops of their feathery stalks. The sun had just begun to dip behind the stunning kaleidoscope landscape, its infinite beauty making her breath snag in her lungs.

Every day she took pleasure in the simple things in life. A bird chirping in the trees was a concert; the wind caressing her skin was silk. Each and every moment had become a miracle.

"Hanna?"

She turned in the direction of Rhune's voice and headed back toward the house. A few yards from the door, she stopped to admire the fresh paint job she and Rhune had applied the day before. The gas station looked nothing like it had two weeks ago. They'd taken down the sign and buried the pumps. Flowers grew in the garden she'd planted alongside the house. Remodeling the interior, however, would need further coaxing. Men! Some were so set in their ways, and changing someone with habits centuries' old wasn't easy, but she was gaining strides every day.

The front door opened without its usual screeching. Another thing she had insisted they fix.

Rhune stood on the porch with a steaming dish in his hands. "My famous tuna casserole."

She grinned. "How famous is it?"

"About a hundred and sixty years. It's actually a legend."

"Well, you haven't poisoned me yet, so I think my chances are pretty good. Plus, I'm immortal, right?"

They laughed as if they'd been together as long as he'd had the recipe. Hanna was happier than she'd ever been. And she didn't suffer one nightmare. At night she accompanied him to Gehenna. Watching what he did no longer affected her. She knew he was doing a gruesome job that needed to be done. The more souls he took, the less evil was left to flourish in the human world.

She kept her promise to never take a soul back once they were committed to Hell. No matter how much they screamed, cried, or prayed, she had to trust in Rhune. And a higher power.

When the night was over and they were back in their bed, he promptly exhausted her the good ol' fashioned way.

As they sat eating dinner, a pang of homesickness set in.

"Something wrong?" Rhune asked around a mouthful of casserole. He reached for her hand.

"Just a little melancholy is all. I miss Darla."

He squeezed her fingers. "You can't go back, you know."

She gave a weak smile and placed down her fork. "Yes, I know. It's just sometimes..."

She was happier than she'd ever been, but there was a part of her that felt guilty about leaving the other world as she'd done.

"Would it help to know that Darla received your old job?"

"A little. Probably making more money than I did too, knowing her."

"I have to confess that digging you up from that grave certainly wasn't one of the highlights of my life."

Hanna remembered waking in that coffin in complete darkness. She had no idea how she could die and then come back to life, but here she was. God did indeed work in mysterious ways.

Rhune and Cerberus had told her the truth. She was a Deathwalker with the ability to return to the mortal world in whatever human form she wanted. She could have chosen to come back as an infant, or looking like Grace Kelly, but Rhune had fallen in love with Hanna Carmichael. If being simple, dowdy Hanna was enough for him, then it was good enough for her.

He'd placed the coffin and dirt exactly as it had been left. No one would ever know she wasn't where she was supposed to be, unless someone else felt inclined to dig her up. The only downside was the scars left by her autopsy. They would remain as constant reminders that life, even for a Deathwalker, is a precious thing.

"Are you lonely?" he asked.

The stricken look on his face made her smile. "No. I'm where I'm supposed to be. Are you? I mean, happy?"

"Happiness doesn't come close to describing how I feel with you here with me. Forever."

When she rose from the table, he pushed his chair back, guided her to his lap, and ran a hand through her hair. His touch made her shiver in the most delightful of ways.

"Well, Rhune, you're a monster, literally, but I love you anyway. I'm going to have moments of homesickness. It's only natural. So I expect you to help me get through them."

He smiled coyly. "It'll be my ultimate pleasure."

"I'm bound to a hellhound. Go figure. But seriously? There's no place I'd rather be in this world— or the next."

The End

About the Author

D. Thomas Jerlo's novels inexplicably draws readers deep into mystical worlds where magic rules and battles between good and evil are forever constant. Blending reality and illusion that leave indelible impacts, readers are riveted to the spellbinding plots and unforgettable characters.

I am enough of an artist to draw freely upon my imagination. Imagination is more important than knowledge. Knowledge is limited. Imagination encircles the world. ~ Albert Einstein

www.dthomasjerlo.com

More Titles from Foundations Publishing Company

Dark Prisoner – The Kruthos Key

By D. Thomas Jerlo

Suna Di'Viao, the last of the Divenean race, has hidden from the world, blaming herself for the demise of King Markes and Queen Saliste. It's a fate she believes she deserves, but when she's summoned on a quest by a mysterious stranger, her Divenean heritage won't allow her to refuse.

EVIN
By A.S. Crowder

Eva has never seen the Forest of Evin, but her fate and the fate of the Forest may be intertwined.

Sinister forces seek to pull the Forest apart, and Eva may be the only one who can save it. Eva must travel between worlds to keep the Forest together...

...but the Forest of Evin thrums with power and the force tearing it apart may not be the only danger.

DECEPTION

By Laura Ranger

Izzy's had a lifetime of liars make up her past. All that changes with Caleb Matthews who's genuine and sincere. He teaches her not all is black or white. After 25 years of marriage she begins to suspect there's more to her husband then what she's known. No matter how she tries, she can't find anything amiss. Is her paranoia from being deceived in her past sabotaging her future or is there something more she's missing?